The Scrambler...

The Life is Good...

But is it Worth it?

KNOWLEDGE PRODUCTIONS
PRESENTS

The
Scrambler...

Copyright © 2004 A Novel by Victorious

Written By Victorious of Victorious Entertainment

ISBN 1-59232-200-X

Gangstabooks.com
PO Box 2085
Long Island City, New York 11102

Printed in the USA

The Scrambler…

A message to the readers:

When I sat down to write this book I had two goals the first was to show spectators on the outside looking in situations inner city youths are faced with. Hopefully after reading this book you will understand the predicaments children in urban city communities endure that make it difficult for them to live up to the expectations that society institute for all children. My second goal was to display to a youth growing up in an inner-city community the results of playing the drug game. A wise man learns from the mistakes of others. Take what you read in this book and apply it to your life. If this book changes one persons perception of a youth growing up in an urban community or helps one child redirect his life out of the drug game my goal will be met. 1000

Thanks for your support,
Victorious

CHAPTER 1

Clinton CF houses all types of criminals murders, rapist, arsonist and scramblers like inmate 96A0395 Anthony "Tony" Clark. Tony had been locked up before but now that his bid was over he realized this one had taken a toll on him.

It was 5:30 am and pitch black in Tony's cell. The God was anxious to get to the streets but he didn't know what to expect. He had spent the last 10 years of his life incarcerated. All he could do is sit and think about his plans he had for his Parole day.

He promised his self that he wouldn't deal with his daughter's mother when he got home. During the time he spent locked up he realized she was the main cause of his down fall. The only problem he had was that he already missed majority of his daughter's childhood, so most importantly he wanted to see his seed.

After Tony's first incarceration he gained the status of Staten Island's Kingpin in the drug game. He knew he could get to the streets and turn it up without a problem but while he was incarcerated he learned of a new hustle. His second mission was to get a street report of who was getting money because he was determined to kill the streets with his new hustle.

Over the years he thought to himself about where in his life did he go wrong. Every time he thought about it he came up with something new. The time seemed to tick while he waited in his cell for his release, so again he started reminiscing about his actions that gave him a second trip up north.

———————

It had to be the coldest day in October when Tony and Tanya walked out the Bowling Green 4 and 5-train station.

"Yo give me the bags, We gotta hurry up we only got two minutes".

"I know Tony but it is cold as shit out here."

The wind whipped their faces as they ran up Broadway trying to catch the 7:30 Staten Island Ferry. While they were running all Tanya could think about was getting to the terminal, so she can feel some heat. As they ran up the steps the doors were starting to close.

While sitting down upstairs on the boat Tanya out of breath,
"Damn we just made it."
"Shit if we would've missed this one we would've had to wait untill 8:00."
"Yo there go your home girl Me-ka."
"Where?"
"Sleep right there next to the door."
"Damn she's knocked out." "Me-ka, Me-ka" Tanya yelled.
She woke up with an attitude but smiled when she seen her home girl Tanya.

Damn she's sexy Tony thought to himself as Me-ka's big breast bounced and thick legs strolled towards them.

"What up yall where yall coming from?"
"I told you in school Tony was taking me to 5th Avenue to cop some Prada's to wear with my outfit."
"You damn sure did."
"Did you decide where you want to go tonight?"

"I wanted to go to the city but it's too cold to go out there."
"I heard there is a party at the Wave tonight."
"Yeah that's where me and my niggas are going" Tony said as he looked at the lip-gloss shining on Me-ka's luscious lips.

"I don't know if I want to fuck with it, you know them Stapelton and Park Hill niggas don't know how to act," Tanya said.

"You right, plus I'm tired of seeing the same-ol-people."
Tony put his headphones on and listened to Jay-Z's Reasonable Doubt album as Tanya and Me-ka continued to have small talk.

As the boat docked Tanya asked Me-ka,
"How you getting home?"
"I was gonna take the bus up."
"Nah jump in the cab with us, it's too cold to wait for the 52."

"You ain't never lie."

They took a De Joy's cab to New Brighton; dropping Me-ka off in front of her building at 61 Jersey Street.

"Call me at like 9:30." Me-ka said as she got out the cab. The cab dropped Tony and Tanya off in the McDonalds houses on the 300th block of Jersey Street.

"Yo your aunt ain't home yet right?"

"Nah."

"Aight, so check it go in the house and I will be over there in a minute."

"Where you going?"

"I'm gonna holler at Ice real quick."

They kissed and went their separate ways.

CHAPTER 2

Tony zipped his NorthFace up and walked up Pauw Street to York Ave. Ice's moms had a nice little crib in the middle of the block. She didn't like Ice's friends ringing her bell, so she hooked up the basement for him. The basement had its own entrance.

Since Ice had his own lab that was basically the hang out for their crew. The door was always open, so Tony walked right in.

"Oh what up nigga?"

"You got lucky. I didn't know who was creeping in here you seen me reach for that thing."

"Nigga what was you reaching for? A belt you ain't got shit."

Everyone started laughing.

Tony shook hands with the familiar faces in his N.F.L. crew (Niggas For Life) and said "What Up" to the unknown faces.

Ice introduced Tony to the unknown faces.

"Yo that's my man Money B," pointing to the dude in the corner. "And that's my man Kareem," pointing to the dude at the pool table.

"Yo this is my man Tony."

"What's good?" The two cats said.

"You still going out with us tonight right? Or you got some homework to do?"

"Nah he gotta go to work in the morning." One of the dudes in his crew yelled out.

As they started laughing

Tony stuck his middle finger up and said, "Yall some funny niggas. Yeah I'm still going out. We still going to the Wave right?"

"Hell yeah we still going that nigga from Park Hill King Just is supposed to be performing, so you know there is gonna be some bitches in there tonight."

"What time we leaving?"

"I'm gonna get dressed as soon as I finish bagging this weed up, I gotta make a couple of drops then we out."

"Aight then I'll be up hear like 10:30-11:00."

Tony walked out the door and headed in the direction of Tanya's aunt's crib. When he reached the corner of her crib he bumped into Sean from the barbershop.

"What's good?"

"Same-o-shit, what up with you?"

"Just trying to get some of that budda from your man Ice. Tell me he's up there."

"Yeah he in there, he bagging up now."

"I wasn't trying to walk all the way up there in the cold and he wasn't there."

"I feel you its cold as shit out here. Yo you cutting tomor-row?"

"Yeah. But you know I only cut by appointments."

"What time can I come through?"

"I got one opening at 9:15 in the morning. Don't be late or I can't cut you."

"Aight I'm there I'll check you in the morning."

They gave each other five and departed.

When Tony finally reached his destination he rang the bell and waited anxiously to get out of the cold.

Tanya finally answered the door.

"Yo what took you so long?"

"I was in the bathroom I didn't hear the bell."

"You was on the phone bumping your gums."

"Whatever."

"Yo who you on the phone with?"

"Me-ka."

"Yall was just on the boat together what is there to talk about already?"

"Yo Me-ka I'm gonna call you back because this nigga is killing me. You happy now I'm off the phone?"

"If I wasn't laying down the pipe I would think yall was fucking."
"Whatever and who said you was laying down anything?"
"Shit you wouldn't be screaming all crazy if I wasn't laying it down."
"I be screaming because I want you to think you doing something."
"Yeah aight. You lucky you got your friend because I would show you right now why you be screaming."

Tanya seeing Tony's man at attention through his sweat pants went in for the kill. She took off her shirt revealing her Red Victoria Secret 34D bra and sat on his lap. Tony palmed her baby soft caramel breast and said,
"Why you playing with me?"
Tanya licking on his neck and speaking in a low seductive tone
"I'm so horny...."
"You still got your friend, stop teasing me."
"Yesterday was my last day."
Hearing that Tony wasted no time he aggressively lifted Tanya off his lap and gently placed her on the sofa. Tony took a second and gazed over Tanya's pure beauty. As Tony laid on top of her desirable body she reached for his erect penis and stroked every inch of his man-ness lubricating it with his pre-discharge.
Tony pulled Tanya's stretch pants down to her ankles and smelled the aroma of fresh Victoria Secrets Vanilla body splash escaping from between her thighs. He had to have a taste...
Tony slowly squatted down to fulfill his thirst. He thought to himself that she definitely had enough to fill his cup. He took one long gulp as Tanya released a deep and passionate roar. She pulled him up towards her and spoke softly "I'm wet enough, put him in."
Tony slowly and gently entered Tanya's warm and saturated vagina; closed his eyes and stroked for what seemed like an eternity. Before either one of them could reach their climax they heard
"Good night Dorothy I will see you in the morning."

CHAPTER 3

Later that evening while Tanya laid her gear out for her night out, her aunt Dorothy walked in the room.

"Tanya can I speak to you for a minute?"

Nervous because of her episode with Tony earlier in the day.

"Yeah what's up?"

"Sit down for a second. You know I treat you like my friend sometimes rather than my niece right?

"Yeah aunt D we cool"

"Alright when I came in from work what was you and Tony doing in the living room?"

"Nothing we were watching a movie."

"Are you sure? You know you can talk to me about any-thing."

"Yeah auntie I'm sure we were watching BELLY."

"I am not accusing you and Tony of anything but I thought yall was having sex. When I walked in you was running to the back, he had a paranoid look on his face and it definitely smelled like yall was doing something."

Tanya stuttering, "Nah I was running in the back because I thought my cell phone was ringing."

Dorothy knowing Tanya was lying raised her voice.

"Tanya stop lying I know yall was fucking in my house. You gonna look me dead in my face and lie like that. I never said that Tony couldn't be in my house while I wasn't home but yall gonna fucking disrespect my house that's fucked up."

Tanya crying, "Auntie we wasn't doing anything."

Screaming while walking out of Tanya's room

"Your little hot ass didn't even make 16 and you out there fucking already. You'll learn when you catch something or get pregnant and you better not let me catch that little motherfucker in my house no more."

Still crying Tanya closed her bedroom-door, laid on her bed and dialed Tony's house; Tony's mother answered.
"Hello Mrs. Clark is Tony home?"
Hearing Tanya sobbing. "Sweet heart he just left out, but are you ok?"
"Yes I am fine."
"Alright then when he comes in I will have him call you."
"Thank you."
Tanya wasting no time called Me-ka's cell phone.
"I'm on my way to your house."
"I'm not going."
"Why what happened?"
"My aunt caught me and Tony fucking earlier."
"What? She walked in on yall, why didn't yall lock the door?"
"Nah we was in the living room when she walked in the house I ran to the back."
"So what did she say?"
"She said she knows we were doing something because she smelled it. She straight screamed on me."
"So she said you couldn't go out?"
"Nah but I don't feel like it now."
"You gotta go out because you're gonna be in the house and all she's gonna do is keep talking about it. My mother was killing me that time she caught me. I'm passing Taft Avenue now; come open the door."

Tony got out a US One cab and tried to walk in Ice's Lab but the door was locked, so he banged on the door.
"Who the fuck is knocking like that?"
"Open the door and find out nigga."
"Why the fuck you banging like the boys?"
"You scared? Why you got the door locked?"
"I definitely ain't scared of your punk ass!"
"We can shoot five than nigga."

"Nigga it ain't nothing but space and opportunity. Hold up your moms let you out on a school night?"

"You stay with jokes. You ready to bounce yet?"

"Yeah just let me throw my shirt on. "Here", throwing Tony the keys, "Go heat the truck up."

After a couple of minutes Ice gets in the truck and they drive off.

"Yo I gotta make a quick stop then we out."

"Aight. Son I seen the bitch Me-ka on the boat today man! That's a sexy bitch."

"Who you telling? Niggas say she be fucking but she ain't fucking nobody in the hood."

"I was fucking my girl today and for a minute I started thinking about her."

"You better chill, Tanya will beat the shit out of you if you slip up and say Me-ka's name.

"I wear the pants."

"Yeah aight don't front for me. Yo I'm gonna get Me-ka watch."

"Nigga your game ain't even like that."

"What! Who bags the most chicks in the crew?"

"You do because I don't be going hard at these chicks."

"That's because you scared of Tanya and before you bagged Tanya I still had the most chicks on my dick."

"That's because these bitches see the Lex Truck and go crazy, you know you a ugly nigga."

Laughing, "Yeah aight nigga."

Coming down St. Paul's Avenue Ice makes a left on Broad Street and they pull in Stapelton projects parking lot behind 218 Broad Street.

"I told this dude to be outside."

"Who?"

"The nigga from my crib earlier Money B."

"What he works for you?"

"Nah he hustles on his own but he fucked some money up, so I'm gonna help him get back on his feet."

"Here he comes now."

Money B approaches the car and sits in the back seat of the truck.

"I knew you wasn't gonna be out here, I was about to leave your ass."

"My fault I seen this chick in the elevator I use to fuck with."

"Take that black book bag."

"Yo good looking. I'm gonna hit you back as soon as I flip twice."

"I ain't sweating it. You going to the club tonight?"

As Money B exits the truck "Yeah I'll see yall over there in a minute."

"Aight chill out."

As they pull out the parking lot and make a right on Broad Street towards Bay Street Tony says,

"That must be your man how you know him?"

"That's a grimy nigga, I just keep him close to me so I can watch him."

"What you mean he's grimy?"

"Man he will do anything to be on top, but his down fall is the bitches. His brother tried to kill him out here one night."

"His brother? For what?"

"His brother found out he fucked his wife."

"Yeah that's a grimy nigga."

"That's why I keep my eye on him."

As they drive up Bay Street and approach the club Ice says,

"You see how packed it's out here already?"

"Yeah it's free for chicks before 12."

"Yo I am gonna park in McDonald's parking lot, you hungry?"

"A little something, shit I didn't eat since I left school."

"Word I gotta eat something before I drink."

Chapter 4

Tanya looked in her bedroom mirror to see how her Chocolate brown suede Prada's looked with the Chocolate brown suede Sean John suit Tony bought her for their Anniversary.

"You can call the cab now, I will be ready in a minute."

"You ain't gonna be ready no time soon."

"All I have to do is comb my wrap out and put on my jacket."

"Yeah hurry up so we can get there before 12."

"You rushing to see the same ol' dudes you seen in lunch today."

"Please I ain't rushing for nobody, it's free before 12. Them niggas are gonna be rushing to see me once they see this body in this leather suit."

"There you go. I don't know why I started you up. Nah but you are killing that suit."

As Me-ka reaches for the phone to call a cab

"I know. You look aight too."

"You are such a hater, you never wanna give me my props."

"The cab said five minutes and excuse me I am too fly to have hate in my blood."

"Whatever, How my butt look in these pants?"

"Like Tony is gonna fuck you up tonight."

Laughing, "Why you say that?"

"Niggas are gonna see your ass and somebody is gonna holler for a Dollar."

With a conceited laugh "My shit looks that good?"

"Laugh now. Tony is gonna fuck you up if he catches you smiling in some nigga face."

"Whatever. Tony knows he's my baby."

"Come on the cab is out there."

As they get in the US One cab Me-ka says,
>"So how was it?"
>"How was what?"
>"You acting funny now? You know I always fill you in when I get my back dug out."

Laughing, "Me-ka I swear you better not say nothing… Tony fucked the shit out of me. With a grin on her face, "It seems like his dick gets bigger every time we have sex."
>"It better had been good your aunt almost beat the shit out of you."
>"I know. I wonder what she's gonna say to Tony when she sees him."

As the cab pulled up to the corner of the Wave Me-ka says,
>"Damn it's packed out here."
>"I know look at that line."

Me-ka paid the cab driver. "Shit we look too good to wait on that line."
>"You ain't never lie."
>"Watch me work my magic to get us in here just follow
me."
>"Aight do you."
>"Fuck it I don't have to work shit, there goes Tony and Ice about to go in with that dude Knowledge from West Brighton."
>"Ice."
>"Who the fuck is out here calling me like that? Oh that's Me-ka and your girl."
>"Tony we in there with yall right?
>"Hold up let me ask my man."
>"Yo Knowledge can you get my girl and her friend in with
us?"
>"Looking like that hell yeah, which one is your girl kid?"

Laughing, "You better stop playing with me."
>"Nah I want the other one."
>"Tell them to come on its cold as shit out here."

Tony talking to Tanya "Yo come on. Knowledge this is my girl Tanya and this is her home girl Me-ka."
>"Nice to meet yall. How old are you Me-Ka?"
>"16."

"Oh no sweet heart they will lock me under the jail for you, but yall go on in and enjoy yourself. Tony I gotta handle something real quick when I'm done I wanna holler at you about something."

"Aight I'll be by the DJ booth."

CHAPTER 5

The four of them enterred the club and Tony spoke.
"Aight yall have fun and Tanya don't get nobody in here fucked up."
"What are you talking about now?"
"Let me catch a nigga in your face and you will find out what I'm talking about."
"Let me catch a chick in your face and the party is gonna be over."
Laughing, "Whatever man we will be by the DJ booth if you need me."
"Aight but later on I gotta talk to you about something."
"Talk to me now."
"Nah it can wait until later."

As they start to walk away Ice catches eye contact with Me-Ka and winks.
"Make sure you save me a dance Me-ka."
Smirking, "You might have to get in line."
"I never wait on lines."
Me-ka smiles and walks away with Tanya.

As Tony and Ice started walking through the crowd they became the center of attention. Tony's baby face and waves spinning in all directions amazed the audience of the club. They paced through the crowd greeting familiar faces. The stroll lights glistened off the diamonds in Ice's chain and earring catching the attention of all hustlers, gold diggers and stick up kids.

They made their way to the bar in the corner. Ice spoke to the bartender who had some sugar in his tank.
"Yo how much is your Moet?"
"If you need to know the price, you can't afford it."

Ice feeling disrespected pulled out two knots.

"I was asking so I knew how much of a tip to give your gay ass."

The dude behind the bar was dazed by how much money Ice had and stuttered.

"IIII…. was only joking."

"Nah I should smack the shit out of your sweet ass."

"I'm sorry. Moet is $50 a bottle."

"Give me two bottles on ice and four glasses."

The bartender sashayed away and came back with Ice's request. Ice gave the bartender $100 and grabbed one of the tubs with Moet in it and Tony grabbed the other one. As they walked away the spectators were stunned how Ice handled the episode.

Across the room Tanya and Me-ka sat and observed people make fools of themselves on the dance floor.

"Yo what was that all about with you and Tony's man Ice?"

"What are you talking about?"

"All that winking and flirting."

"It ain't nothing you know I have to be nice to my fans."

"Its something, you usually shut dudes down right away."
Smiling, "Whatever."

"You feeling him ain't you?"

"I mean he hollered at me before but you know I don't fuck with New Brighton niggas."

"Here you go. Why not?"

"Because I'm from the New and they are too close to home."

"And?"

"You know everybody's fucking everybody in New Brighton plus chicks be hating."

"You ain't never lie! Fuck them chicks if you feeling him do you."

As Tanya was finishing her sentence Money B approached them.

"Me-ka what's going on?"

"Hey Money B how you doing?"

"Shit I'm chilling what's up with your brother?"

"He's cool he's playing ball in Portland now."

"That's cool as long as he's getting that money, who's this?

"My fault this is my home girl Tanya. Tanya this is Money B."

Money B sticks his hand out and kisses Tanya's hand. He passionately looks in her eyes

"Nice to meet you."

Tanya smiles. "Same here."

"Aight Me-Ka I'll see yall later on."

Money B walked away looking back at Tanya.

"Hold up. You talking about me what was that all about?"

"What?"

"All that sexy look in your eyes and same here shit."

"What are you talking about you introduced us and I shook his hand."

"Aight. You lucky Tony didn't see that shit."

"Whatever all I did was shake the dudes hand."

"You know Tony would not try to hear that."

"Anyway are you gonna mess with Ice or what?"

"I like how you changed the subject but I don't know I gotta see how he acts tonight?"

"I haven't seen them since we got here."

"I see you checking on your man."

"You know I don't trust these bitches plus you know he's sneaky."

"Lets go on the dance floor and see if we see them."

"Come on."

They walked through the crowded dance floor looking for Tony and Ice, while dudes on the dance floor tried to stop them to dance.

"Tanya do you see them yet?"

"Nah not yet."

"Oh look at this shit."

"What?"

"There they go over there." Pointing in the direction of the DJ booth."

"They know each other?"

"I knew Money B knew Ice, but I didn't know Tony knew him?"

"He probably doesn't know Tony. He's probably over there with Ice."

"Who else is that over there with them?"

"That's Ice, Tony, Money B, and Dramah."

"Who's Dramah?"

"You know Dramah from New Brighton. He just came home."

"Nah I don't know him."

"Yes you do. He used to Box back in the day."

CHAPTER 6

"Oh shit what's the science God?"
"Same shit on my end."
"Dramah how long you been home?"
"Today made a week."

"Yo Money B why you didn't tell me the God was home?"
"Shit I seen him for the first time after I left you in Stapelton.
The God asked for you so I told him you would be in here."
"Fuck it Dramah you trying to drink?"
"Nah the kid is natural. I'm about to get back in the ring."
"God you still got it or you playing?"
"I ain't never lose it. Why you think I been on the low? I been
in the gym getting right."
"Oh pardon me. You know my man Tony right?"
"Yeah I know his face. He was a young dude when I was
home. Peace God." Giving Tony a five.
"Peace."

Knowledge keeps his eye on them conversing from across the
room
Thinking to himself,
    "I don't trust that little grimy nigga Money B. I gotta warn this
nigga Tony." He walked through the crowd and approached their
huddle.
    "Yo Tony let me holler at you real quick."
    "Yeah what up?" as they walk off from the huddle.
    "Yo you know you me and my man are just looking out for
you. I know you're your own man and you gonna do what
you want, but watch yourself around that nigga Money B."
    "Yeah you the second person to tell me that. My man Ice
told me the same thing."
    "Ice told you that?"

"Yeah."

"So why the fuck is he playing the nigga close in here?"

"He knows the nigga is grimy he just keeping the nigga close, so he could keep his eye on him."

"Nah I don't believe that shit at all. Think about it if you knew a nigga was grimy and he be setting hustlers up why would you have the nigga in your circle?"

"Yeah you right about that."

"Yo you hustling?

"Nah why you say that?"

"Nigga you doing something. Ice and Money B hustle you ain't with them for no reason."

"Nah Ice is my man I was fucking with him before he started hustling and we seen Money B in here."

"Yo this hustling shit ain't for you I wish I never got into this shit but thats all I know."

"I feel you."

"I'm telling you, you got your little chick just keep going to school and do you. You're gonna be the one that makes it out the hood."

"Yeah you right I'm almost done with school too."

"See that's good. I know Ice is your man and all, but you need to keep it light with him. You don't need to get caught up in the game."

"Yo there are some bad bitches in here."

"You ain't lying."

"Yo Ice I'm about to bag this little bad chick in here."

"Yeah what see look like? She's probably one of my joints."

"Nah she is out of your league. I seen her with shorty from your hood."

"If she from my hood she definitely one of mines. Who was she with?"

"She was with the kid Omar that play ball little sister."

"Hold up what she look like?"

"She's tall, brown skin, her hair came to like her shoulders. I'm telling you shorty is official."

"I think that's my man's chick. Did she have on a brown outfit with some brown Prada's?"

"Yeah that's her."

"Nah chill that's my man Tony's girl."

"Who the nigga that was just with you?"

"Yeah."

"God is that his girl or he just fuck with her because when Me-Ka introduced us she was smiling all in my face."

"You sure? Because that's the kids wife and she be shutting niggas down for him."

"I'm telling you she was looking all in my eyes and smiling."

"Just chill for now. Let me see if they still fuck with each other."

"Nah she's feeling me you know how I get down. If she fuck with him or not I'm gonna holler."

"Son just do me that favor. Chill and let me see what's good. Here he comes now don't mention it too him"

As Tony approaches them they stop talking, but he notices something is up.

"Yo what's good? What was yall niggas talking about?"

"Nothing. What this nigga Knowledge wanted?"

"Shit he was just asking me about school and seeing if I still worked at the movies."

"Oh aight. Yo you ready to slide out of here?"

"Fuck it whenever you ready I gotta get a cut in the morning anyway."

"Aight ask Me-Ka and them if they need a ride and I'll meet you at the door."

"Smooth. Money B chill out."

As Tony reaches to give Money B five Money B looks away and gives Tony a fishy five. Tony doesn't take notice to it and walks away.

"Yo what's all that about?"

"What?"

"Why you give him a shady five like that?"

"That ain't my man like that."

"Son earlier everything was peace now that you wanna fuck with his girl you acting funny."

"His girl wanna fuck with me."

"Check it, you're my man and he's my man do me that favor and leave his shorty alone. I'm gonna find out if he stills messes with her if not than do you."

"Aight."

"I'm gone. Give the nigga Dramah my math and tell him to get at me."

"When I see him tomorrow I'm gonna give him your numbers."

"Good looking 1,000."

Ice walks through the audience admiring his jewelry and heads for the door. He sees Tony, Me-Ka and Tanya at the door waiting for him. Me-Ka speaks first as they walk out the club.

"Hey Ice you sure you're ready to leave you have a lot of admirers in here."

"I'm not worried about them only person I'm worried about is you."

"So you say."

"I'm for real. Yo what happened to my dance?"

"Please you were too busy. I didn't see you all night."

"You had too many dudes trying to holler."

"I wasn't worried about none of them I was waiting for you to holler."

"Yo Tanya your home girl got game."

As they reach Ice's truck "Ice who you telling? Yo Me-Ka sit up front I wanna talk to Tony."

On the ride home Ice and Me-Ka continued to flirt with each other while Tony and Tanya sat in the back and discussed Tanya's episode with her aunt about their sexual encounter. They reached New Brighton.

"Tone you want me to drop you off at Tanya's house or you going home?"

"Drop her off I want to make sure she gets in the crib then you can drop me off."

"Yall want me to stop at the store or yall good?"

"Nah we cool you can just drop us off."

Tony drove down Jersey Street and pulled over when he reached Hendricks Ave to let Tanya out.

"Alright yall. Thanks for the ride Ice."

"No problem. Yo Tanya you hurt them tonight with that outfit."

"Thanks but your boy picked it out."

"Don't give that nigga all the credit."

"Aight good night yall. Me-Ka call me in the morning."

"Aight."

"Yo Ice hold up I'll be right back let me walk her to the door."

" Yeah."

When Tony got back in the car Ice drove down Jersey Street and made a right on Crescent Ave to drop Tony off at his crib across the street from Mahony Park.

"Ice good looking."

"No question. What's good for tomorrow?"

"I'm going to see Sean at the shop in the morning then I gotta work till six after that whatever."

"Aight then holler at me when you get home we'll do something."

"Aight. Good night Me-Ka."

"Bye Tony."

Chapter 7

"What's up Me-ka you gonna come chill with me?"
"It is 4:30 in the morning where the hell we going right now?"
"What you got a curfew or something?"
"You trying to play me?"
"Nah I got my own crib we can go to my crib."
"So you had this all planned out? You dropped them off first, so you can get me by myself."
Laughing, "Nah you thinking too hard, so you gonna come chill with me or what?"
"Ice can I trust you?"
"Yeah you can trust me."
"Aight then. I'll chill with you for a little while."

Ice pulled off and drove in the direction of his house. He parked on the corner of his block and they walked to his bachelors pad.
"I hope none of your girls are in the house waiting for you."
"There you go. I see you stay with jokes."
"I speak the truth."

They entered Ice's apartment.
"Make yourself at home."
"You sure you don't want me to stand here while you hide your chicks pictures?"
"Nah I did that before I left."
"So you knew you was gonna bring someone home?"
"You're not gonna let me win are you?"
"Can't handle the pressure?"
"Whatever. You can have a seat on the couch if you like."
"Thank you."
"You can see if something is on TV or you can put in a DVD."

"So you're a gentleman huh?

"A gangster and a gentleman."

"You think you're Styles P?"

"Nah it's true I'm a gangster, but I know how to treat a lady."

"Till you get what you want."

"I don't have any motives. Anyway would you like something to drink?"

"Yes I'll have something."

"You want a real drink or you want some juice?"

"What's a real drink?"

"I have a full bar."

"Excuse me baller. I will have a sex on the beach."

"I didn't say I was a bartender. I have liquor. I don't know how to mix drinks."

"Alright so I have something light, you pick it."

"I'll pick the drink you pick the DVD."

Ice walked to the bar and mixed two Absolute Vodka's with cranberry juice, while Me-Ka picked out Drum Line for them to watch. Ice gave Me-Ka her drink then turned off the lights and lit a candle. They relaxed on Ice's soft leather sofa and watched Drum Line, while the effects of the Absolute Vodka took over. The aroma of Me-Ka's Iceberg Twice perfume stimulated Ice's hormones. Lying between Ice's legs Me-Ka felt his penis starting to stiffen which made her vagina become moist. Ice realizing Me-ka felt his manhood standing at attention.

"Yo you can't lay like that no more."

"Why?"

"You know why."

Smiling, in an enticing tone "I got that effect on you?"

"Don't give yourself that much credit."

"So how much credit should I give myself?"

Walking towards his pool table "You in here playing around, you know how to play pool?"

Following Ice "Yeah I know how to play, the question is do you know how to use the stick?

Handing Me-Ka a stick. "Believe me I know how to use the stick but do you know how to make the balls go in the hole?"

Taking the first shot at the balls "There's only one way to find out."

Surprised by Me-Ka's comments. "I'm willing to find out."

Me-Ka bending over facing Ice revealing cleavage.
          "Let's be serious you know you can't handle all this."
Running her hands all over her body.

          "I'm tired of you trying to play me."Wwalking around the
pool table and grabbing Me-Ka.

Gazing directly in Ice's eyes.
          "So you're not scared to touch me"

Ice pulled Me-ka closer to him, wrapped his arm around her waste
and began to caress Me-Ka's earlobe with his tongue. Me-ka
enjoying his touch began to quiver and relaxed against the pool
table. With his hormones electrifying he took one hand and began
to unbuttoned Me-Ka's leather shirt and took his other hand and
placed her hand on his cock. Surprised by the bulk in her hand,
she pulls the drawstrings of his sweat pants and reveals his
manhood then says, "Lay on the table". Without procrastination
Ice stepped out of his sweat suit and laid on the carpet of the pool
table. "I know you heard about my head game."
"I never heard but I'm ready to find out" Me-Ka smiled grasped his
cock in her right hand, closed her eyes and drenched it with the
salivation of her mouth. His eyes rolled to the back of his head,
toes curled and thought to himself "her shit is official". Me-Ka's
head nodded up and down until he sighed and she felt babies
playing in the back of her throat. Ice laid on the pool table trembling
while Me-Ka took off her shirt and walked to the bathroom to spit.
On Me-Ka's walk back she thought to herself "this nigga better
have condoms."
As Me-Ka strolled back to the pool table Ice examined Me-Ka's
breast bounce with every-one of her steps.
          "How's my head game?"
          "Official."
Ice sprung from the pool table freed Me-Ka's breast from her bra
and licked her chocolate deluxe breast and sucked her milk dud
nipples. She enjoyed every lick and suck placing one hand on the

back of his head. He then placed his hand on her throbbing vagina while she spoke with an erotic tone.

"She's all yours."

"Take them tight ass pants off."

"You got condoms?"

"Yeah take them off and I'll get them."

Ice walks off. Me-Ka fought to get her leather pants off, as she finally gets them down she places her hand into her boy shorts and fondles her clitoris. Ice returns and sees her masturbating.

"Yeah that's sexy."

" You got the condoms?"

"Yeah."

"What kind are they?"

"Magnums."

"Let me put it on for you."

Ice handed her the condom out of the wrapper.

"Do you."

Me-Ka put the condom in her mouth bent over and rolled the condom over his cock without using her hands. Ice smiled.

"You're a pro."

Me-Ka positioned herself against the pool table in a doggy style pose.

Ice grabbed his cock in his hand to insert himself into her. He thought to himself "I better not strike out." Me-Ka looked back at him and seen a nervous look on his face. "Put your seat belt on its gonna be a bumpy ride." and smiled. That did nothing for Ice but build his confidence up. He slid inside her deep and throbbing womb and penetrated her insides, while Me-Ka stretched for an object to hold on to. They enjoyed each others thrust throughout the early morning and completed there sex-a-thon with a joint orgasm.

CHAPTER 8

"What up yall?" Tony greeted the dudes in the barbershop.

"Yeah I see you on time for once."

"Sean I'm on time, so that means I'm next right?"

"Nah I got three heads in front of you."

"Why the hell do you give out appointments than?"

"My fault we opened up late."

"Damn I gotta go to work, so what time can I come back later?"

As a dude was getting out of Sean's chair.

"This nigga about to cry I'm fucking with you nigga get in the chair."

"You a clown you always playing."

As Sean brushed Tony's 360's.

"Yo you went to the Wave last night?"

"Yeah that shit was aight."

"You was in there when them niggas was shooting?"

"Nah. Me and Ice broke out like 4:00/ 4:15."

"You still want me to keep it dark right?"

"Yeah."

"Yall must've got out of there just in time."

"Word. Who was shooting?"

"You know when niggas get that Hennessy in their system they don't know how to act. I heard some kid named Money B or something like that from Stapelton was letting off.

"Word I seen him in there too. Anybody got popped?"

"Nah, but some girl got trampled."

"Damn that's crazy."

"Yeah that's why I don't be fucking with the Wave."

"I feel you. How Bones doing?"

"She aight. Yo you still go to Curtis right?"

"Yeah I graduate this year."

As he began to line up Tony's hairline "That's good kid. You going to college?"

"I was thinking about it but I'm not trying to go far."

"You might as well ain't shit out here."

"Shit I never been away from the hood."

"You got the chance kid. Niggas are getting popped and locked up everyday."

Tony rose from the chair "You ain't never lie."

"I'm telling you. You ain't missing shit out here."

Tony paid Sean and gave him a five "I hear you. Yo I gotta go to work. I'm gonna holler at you though."

"Good looking but think about what I said."

"Aight yall niggas be easy." He exited the barbershop and walked to the corner and waited for the 62 bus to go the United Artist Theater.

"Hello may I speak to Tanya please?"

"Hold on."

"Hello."

"Tanya what up?"

"Nothing chilling. What up with you?"

"Trying to recover."

"Recover from what? You had one drink last night."

"Not from liquor."

Laughing. "Hold up. Where did you go when you left me this morning?"

Unconvincingly. "I went home."

"You're lying I hear it in your voice. Where did you go?"

Laughing uncontrollable "Nah I chilled with Ice."

"You fucked him didn't you?"

"Why you say that?"

"Because I know you."

"Yeah I fucked him."

"You're a hoe."

"How am I a hoe?"

"You fucked him within hours."

"I got drunk and then..."

"And then what you fucked him?"

"Nah he fucked me."

Smiling "It was like that?"

Scandalously "Yeah all that. His shit was in my stomach and he had stamina"

"Listen to you. You're sprung."

"Off that I can't even lie."

"So yall go out now?"

"Nah I told him I'm gonna do me."

"He told you that or you told him that?"

"I told him that."

"You confirmed it. You're a hoe."

"Fuck you. Why you say that?"

"You fucked him than told him to do him. That right there is hoeish."

"I can't fuck with him. His dick is too good."

"And?"

"That's too much drama for me. Bitches he fuck with will die for that dick."

"You just using that as an excuse to do you."

"You think I'm playing I don't mess with niggas whose pipe game is that official."

"So you like little dick dudes?"

"Nah I rather teach a nigga how I like it and then dis him." Snickering. "You kill me everyday. What he said when you told him that you was gonna do you?"

"I seen it in his face he was fucked up, but he tried to play it off and say he respects that."

"You gonna have him thinking he was wack."

"Nah the way I was in there hollering he knows he did the damn thing."

"That shit must run in their crew because I told you Tony shit is unbelievable."

"The name of their crew is N.F.L right?"

"Yeah."

"That shit must stand for Niggas are Fucking Long." Giggling "You are stupid. What you doing today?"

"That damn club got my hair smelling like smoke. I want to go get a wash and set, but I probably do it myself."

"Stop lying. Ice sweated that shit out."

Smirking, "Yeah that to, but I need it done. Your aunt still talking about you and Tony."

"Nah I was in the kitchen with her this morning. She didn't mention it."

"That's good. My mother talked about that shit for a month straight"

"You going out with Tony tonight?"

"I don't know he's at work right now. I guess he'll call me when he gets off."

"If yall don't do anything lets go to the movies."

"Alright. I'll call you when I find out."

"Aight. I'll talk to you later."

Click on both ends.

When Tony stepped off the 62 bus later that evening he looked around and admired the run down houses and sanitation depart-ment on Jersey Street and Victory Boulevard. The words that Sean and Knowledge spoke to him rang in his head "there ain't shit out here". As Tony reached the 24-hour store on Jersey Street and Brighton Avenue TNT had three dudes against the store window directing a so-called routine shake down.

Tony spoke to himself

"Yeah this shit must be a sign or some shit. I gotta get the fuck out of here. I hate these fucking pigs."

Approaching Tanya's house he contemplated if he should knock on her door or call her from Ice's house. Realizing today was Satur-day and knowing Dorothy didn't work on the weekends he ex-cepted the latter. He arrived at Ice's crib and walked in as if he lived there.

"You keep walking in here like my thing don't go off."

Taking a seat next to Ice on the sofa "Whatever nigga. What up?"

Giving Tony a five. "Same shit. You just got off of work?"

"Yeah. I see it's hot out there today."

"What the boys is out there?"

"Yeah when I was walking down they was searching some dudes in front of the 24-hour store."

"That's what them niggas get. They stand in front of that store all day long and make hand to hand sales."

"Now that you say that, them niggas was up there when I walked to the barbershop this morning."

"I bet you if we ride by there right now there is a new set of niggas up there. They be making that store hot."

"Fuck it. Let me use your jack real quick."

"The cordless is on my bed."

Walking towards Ice's bed. "You know I gotta call my hoes."

"Stop fronting. You know you about to call Tanya."

Dialing the number "Yeah her aunt ain't fucking with me."

"That was your home girl what happened?"

"I'm gonna tell you when I get off the phone."

"No I gotta tell you something when you get off the phone."

Tony began to talk to Tanya while Ice looked in his walk-in closet to look for an outfit to throw on for the day. He hardly wore an outfit twice, so it took him a while to approve of a combination. When Tony hung up the phone he excitedly called Ice's name.

"What nigga?"

"You're a funny nigga."

"What you talking about?"

"You know exactly what I'm talking about."

Smirking "Tanya told you."

"Yeah she told me. How the fuck did you pull that off?"

"Shit we was in here chilling, we started drinking and shit than it went down."

"Oh you don't get no points for that she was drunk."

"Nah it was gonna go down regardless. She was on my dick before she got drunk."

"How was it?"

"My nigga I'm not even exaggerating that had to be the best pussy I ever had."

Smiling, "She got you open."

"I can't even front kid I was thinking about that ass all day today."

"Tell me she used them big ass lips of hers."

"God the head game is official."

Energized, "Nigga You lying."

"God she's a professional. She put a condom on my dick with her mouth and she didn't use her hands."

"I know that shit fucked you up."

"I almost nutted when I seen that shit."

Giving Ice a five, "You did say you was gonna fuck her."

"I can't even front. I was surprised I fucked her so fast".

Making hand gestures. "Son her titties are so soft and she got some big ass nipples. When I was sucking her shits I just knew I was gonna nut."

"Yo chill out before you nut now."

Laughing, "Nah I'm telling you her shit is official.

"Fuck it. What's good for tonight?"

"I can't call it. Yo you heard about your man Money B?"

"You talking about last night?"

"Yeah I heard the nigga was letting off when we left."

"I talked to him earlier. He said some kids from the Harbor tried to front on him."

"I heard his street report is crazy."

"Yeah the dude got a lot of enemies, that's why I try not to be in the streets with him. I'll meet him some where or he'll come through here for a minute and be out."

"Son make sure you're on point. Don't get caught up in that nigga shit."

"Who you telling?"

"Yo my girl and Me-Ka are going to the movies. I'm not trying to go back out there I seen every movie out. So what's good?"

"Fuck it lets go get something to eat. We can come back here and chill."

"What you trying to eat?"

"I want to sit down and eat. Lets go to Perkins."

"I feel you. You're ready now or you want to wait?"

"Yeah we can be out now I'm starving."

Chapter 9
Three Months Later

January 15th; Me-Ka stands in front of Curtis High School drinking a hot chocolate trying to eliminate the cold air that is whistling up Hamilton Ave. She stands there waiting for 9th period to end, so she could accompany Tanya to the HIP center. A Honda Accord with tinted windows stops across the street from her and beeps the horn. Me-Ka not recognizing the car pays it no mind and goes back to fighting the wind. The window roles down and sitting in the driver seat was Money B. Distinguishing his face she walks over to the car.

"Oh so you don't know me now?"
Laughing "Stop tripping you know it ain't like that. I couldn't see in the car."
"So you say. What you doing standing out here in the cold?"
"I'm waiting for my home girl to get out of class."
"Oh I thought times was hard and you was out here doing something strange for a piece of change."

Sucking her teeth, "You play to much."
"Nah I'm just playing. Who you waiting for my girl friend?"
"Who's your girlfriend?"
"Shorty that was in the Wave with you that night."
"Tanya? Please boy she is married."
" What that mean? Plug me in with her."
"She ain't thinking about nobody but her man."
"She still mess with school boy?"
"There you go. How you know she mess with Tony?"

"I did my homework."
Smirking "If you really did your homework you would know she ain't

trying to hear nobody."

"We will see. Pointing across the street. "There she goes right there. Tell her to come here."

Me-Ka screaming to grab her attention.
"TANYA."

Tanya walked across the street to the car with a feverish look on her face.
"Tanya you aight."
"Yeah I'm aight. I'm just tired."
"You remember Money B right?"
"Yeah. Hi."
"Its nice to see you again."
"Same here."
"I'm sorry to rush yall but Me-Ka we have to be there at 3:30."
"Yall need a ride somewhere?"
Tanya spoke up before Me-ka could except his offer. "No thank you we're going to take the bus."
"Its Jack Frost out here. Let me at least give yall a ride to the shelter."
Me-ka who was freezing from waiting on Tanya expeditiously answered. "Yes you can give us a ride to the shelter."
"Aight. Get in then, so yall won't miss the bus."
Me-ka walked around to the passenger's side and got in. Tanya got in the car and sat directly behind Money B. Money B fixed his rear view mirror so he could examine Tanya's beauty. It was a silent ride from Curtis to the shelter. Money B wanted to converse, but the look on Tanya's face cautioned him not to speak a word. When they arrived at the shelter they thanked him for the ride and they exited the car. Money B knew he didn't see them too often, so this may be his only chance to holler at Tanya. He rolled down the window and caught eye contact with Me-Ka.
"Yo come here real quick."
"What up?"
"Do me a favor you got my number right?"
"You know I never had your number."
"Aight. Here give this to Tanya and tell her to get at me."

"She is not going to call you. I already told you she has a man."

"Nah just tell her I want to be her friend."

"Here goes my bus. I'm going to give her the number if she calls she calls if not there ain't nothing I can do."

"Aight good looking."

Me-ka walked away joined Tanya as they get on the 61 bus and sat down in the middle of the bus.

Passing Tanya Money B's number.

"Here."

Looking on the back of the business card.

"What am I supposed to do with this?"

"I can't call it. I told him I would give it to you."

"That's what he called you to the car for?"

"Yeah. I told him you had a man. He said he just wants to be your friend."

Blushing. "Typical."

"Anyway how you feeling?"

"I feel better now, but this morning I was throwing up crazy."

"Did your aunt hear you?"

"She stayed at her boyfriend's house last night."

"Did you tell Tony yet?"

"You still the only person I told."

"I almost slipped up and told Ice last night."

Excitedly "What? Tell the truth did you tell him?"

"Nah."

"So how did you almost tell him?"

"We was talking and I asked him his middle name. He told me and I was like that's a nice name to name Tanya's baby."

"So you did tell him?"

"Nah he asked me if you was pregnant. I fixed it up and said no, I'm never having kids so when Tanya has kids that'll be a nice name. He believed me so you have nothing to worry about."

"So yall had this conversation before or after he blew your back out?"

"Before. After we do the damn thing I go right to sleep."

"I hope you ain't fucking him raw."

"I can't even front. I did once."

"You better chill out. You're gonna be knocked up just like me."

"Nah I'm good I'm never having kids."

"Never say never. I said the same thing."

"Nah I like too many expensive things to have kids."

"We're getting off the next stop."

Tanya rang the bell. They got off the bus on Clove Road and walked in the blistering cold up the street to the HIP center.

CHAPTER 10

Ice lounged in his lab counting the days profits, as one of his soldiers sat in eyes distance and bagged up tomorrows high for the smokers in the street. They both were interrupted by a knock at the door.

"Yo check the window and see who that is."

"That's your man Money B."

"Leave that nigga out there. First put that weed in the cabinet then you can open it."

Ice's soldier secured all the weed than opened the door. Money B walked in surprised to see someone else there with Ice. Walking towards Ice   "Yo what took yall niggas so long to open the door?"

Giving Money B a five "Shit I was sleep. He had to wake me up to get the ok to let your ass in."

"Somebody after you? You usually got the door opened."

"Nah the boys are out there kid."

"I feel you. Let me get two twenties from you."

"I ain't got shit I'm waiting now for my man to call me."

"Damn what time you think you'll have that?"

"I can't call it. You're like the 10th person who came through here."

"Hit me on my cell when your man gets at you."

Money B got up and walked towards the door. As he reached for the knob Tony walked in from work. Money B not expecting his entry jumped back in amazement.

"Damn nigga you scared the shit out of me."

Laughing   "My fault. What up though?"

"Same shit. I seen your girl today."

"Oh word where at?"

"I was driving by the shelter and I seen her and Me-Ka.
Hold up where you coming from in that uniform?"
"From work."
Clowning Tony "Where the fuck you work at?"
"The UA."

"Yo Ice you need to put your man on."
"Nah he's good."

Turning back to Tony "Son if you want a bomb just let me know."
"Nah I'm good."
"God you can't be that good working minimum wage."

Ice realized Tony was getting aggravated so he cut Money B off.
"Yo Money I told you the nigga was good. Let him be."
"Aight. I'm gone. Make sure you get at me when you hear
from your man.

Money B looked at Tony smiled and shook his head as he walked
out of Ice's apartment.

"God you aight?"
"Yeah I'm good. Your man got me heated."
"Fuck that nigga get that money your way."
"That nigga tried to play me."
"Don't even sweat it."

Ice's soldier spoke up.
"Yo why didn't you give him the weed?"
"Son I don't sell shit until I'm finished bagging up; especially
to that nigga. If he would've seen all that work on the table
he probably would've tried to send one of them stick up kids
in here. Matter of fact, lock that door and finish bagging
up."

"Yo I'm sick right now. That nigga tried to play me."
"Son I told you don't sweat it. He ain't even getting money
like that. He's been hustling for years and the nigga is still
doing hand to hands in Stapelton."
"Get the fuck out of here."

"That's word."

"He tried to play me and he's still nickel and dimming. Fuck him I ain't even sweating it."

Dorothy came home from a long day at work. She sat in her bedroom and performed her daily routine of eating dinner and talking on the phone all night until falling asleep. While on the phone with her boyfriend she received a call waiting call.

"Hello."

"You have a collect call from. Diane. An inmate in a state correctional facility to except these charges press 5 now, otherwise if you do not except hang up now."

"I hope she don't think I'm gonna be three waying people tonight." Pressing the number 5 on the phone.

"You may go ahead now."

"Hello."

"Hey Dorothy. Thanks for excepting. I'm not going to keep you long I'm just calling to see how Tanya is doing."

"If you only knew."

"Why? What happened?"

"That girl thinks she is grown. She's 16 going on 22."

"She's giving you a hard time?"

"No not really, but I know she's out there having sex with her little boyfriend."

"She wrote me about some little boy named Tony. That's who you talking about?"

"Yeah that's him. I caught them in here having sex a couple of months ago."

"Hey Dorothy I'm sorry. I appreciate you taking care of my daughter while I'm in here. I have five more months left please just hold on to her for me."

"Listen Diane you are my little sister, you don't have to worry about Tanya. I will look after her as long as she stays in school and doesn't come in here pregnant."

"Thank you sis I owe you my life. I'm going to let you go. Do me a favor tell Tanya I called and I love her. I'm gonna write her as soon as I hang up the phone with you."

"I will."

"Thanks again Dorothy. I love you and I will talk to you later."

"I love you too. Bye."

Dorothy hung up the phone called her boyfriend back and continued her daily routine.

CHAPTER 11

Tanya and Me-Ka traveled home from the doctor's office in tranquility. Me-Ka knew something was wrong, but she didn't know if Tanya felt comfortable talking about it. As they reached New Brighton Tanya broke the silence.

"Me-ka can you call Ice for me and see if Tony is with him?"

"Yeah I hope my battery is not dead."

Me-Ka reached in her bag for her phone and called Ice.

"Peace who this?"

"Stop fronting you know who this is."

"Here we go again. Nah what up sexy?"

"Whatever. Is your home boy with you?"

"Who Tone?"

"Who else would I be asking for?"

"Yeah he right here."

"Put him on the phone Tanya wants to speak to him."

"Hold on. Yo Tone your girl wants you."

"What up sweety?"

"Tony I have to speak to you."

"Damn. How was your day? Mine was good."

"Tony stop playing for real I have to speak to you."

"I'm on the phone go ahead."

Tanya speaking with an annoyed tone. "No I have to speak to you when it's just me and you."

Tony hears the seriousness in her voice. "Ma what's wrong?"

"Nothing. I just have to speak to you."

"Aight. Where you at now?"

"On my way home."

"Your aunt is in the crib right?"

"Yeah."

"I'm going home now, so meet me at my house."
"No. I'm almost home meet me on Layton Ave and we can walk to your house together."
"Aight don't have me waiting out there forever."
"Bye."

Tony hung up the phone and swiftly put his North Face on. Ice seeing the nervous look on Tony's face inquired about his phone call.

"Yo what happened?"
"I don't know. She wouldn't tell me. She just kept saying I tell you when I see you."
"Slow down nigga. Chill out you know it ain't no chick saying she fuck with you."
"Why you say that?"
"Tanya knows she is the only chick you fucked with since junior high school."
"Whatever nigga I'm out."
"Son hit me if you need something."
"Aight 1."

Tony walked down the street with his mind in so many different places he didn't see the Mercedes Benz truck pull up on the side of him. He jumped when the driver beeped the horn.

"Oh shit. Great God you scared the shit out of me."
"God you better be aware of your surroundings out here."
"I feel you."
"Yo you need a ride somewhere?"
"Nah I'm about to meet my girl at the bottom of the hill."
"Her and Me-Ka are on their way down I just rode past them."
"Yeah."
"Aight then I'll holler at you. You better stay alert 1000."

As Great God drove off Tony spoke to himself.

"Damn I'm tripping. I damn sure didn't see him pull up on me. I wonder what the fuck is so important."

When Tony reached the bottom of the hill Tanya and Me-Ka stood on the corner awaiting his arrival.

"It took you long enough." Me-Ka joked.

"Whatever yall must've been running down the block."

He walked towards Tanya and gave her a hug and kiss. He saw the vexed expression on her face, so he used his judgment not to ask her what was wrong in front of Me-Ka. He didn't know if her response would be embarrassing. They began to walk in the direction of Tony's crib. When they reached the corner of Tony's block Me-Ka departed while Tanya and Tony continued to his house in silence.

They both sat down on his mattress. Tony being so eager to find out what was troubling her asked her the question before he could take off his coat.

"Tanya what's the problem?"

"There ain't no problem."

"So what did you have to speak to me about?"

Tears beginning to formulate in her eyes she spoke with a shattering tone.   "I don't know how to tell you."

"Tell me what?"

Shaking her head.

The thought of her cheating crossed his mind as he spoke with an elevated pitch.

"Tell me what?"

"Stop yelling."

"So what do you have to tell me?"

"I'm pregnant."

Placing his arm around Tanya to console her while wiping her face of teardrops running down her cheeks.

"Everything is gonna be aight."

Sobbing. "For you. What am I going to tell my aunt?"

Caressing her back. "What you mean what are you going to tell her?"

"She told me don't come in her house pregnant."

"Fuck it don't tell her shit yet. We got some time we will figure something out."

"Tony I'm about to start showing if I don't tell her she is really going to flip."

"When did you find out you was pregnant?"

Hesitant to answer the question.   "I knew something was wrong I didn't get my period for a month in a half, so I went to my GYN and she told me I was pregnant."

Recognizing something was up he discontinued caressing her back and stood up. "That's not what I asked you."

"For a little while."

Raising his voice "Tanya stop fucking playing with me. How long did you know you was pregnant?"

"Why do you always have to curse?"

"Because I always have to ask you shit three and four times. Now how long did you know you was pregnant?"

Lowering her head and speaking in a soft tone. "Two months"

"Don't fucking speak low now speak up."

"I said two months."

"Why the fuck am I just finding out?"

"I didn't know how to tell you."

"I bet you knew how to tell fucking Me-Ka."

Tears pouring from her eyes she sat on the bed with a lost of words

"Oh so a cat got your tongue now?"

"No."

"Does Me-Ka know or not?"

"She took me to the doctor."

"That's some bullshit you can tell me everybody else's business but you can't tell me that you're pregnant."

Entering a depressed state "I'm sorry Tony."

"Nah you got me sick right now."

"That's why I didn't want to tell you in the first place."

"Get the fuck out of here don't try to put it on me. If you would've told me in the first place I wouldn't be sick."

Tanya placed her head in her hands and continued to cry while

Tony looked out his window blazing with anger. Tony thought about the situation and realized he had over reacted. He walked back to the bed and placed her in his arms.

"Listen ma I'm sorry for all that. You know that's not even my style."

"I know."

"I was heated about some shit that happened earlier and when you told me that it just mad me explode. I'm sorry aight."

Drying her tears with his shirt "Yeah."

"Listen everything will work out aight."

"But what am I going to tell my aunt?"

"Just tell her and see what she says."

"It sounds good, but I know she is going to beef."

"You want me to be there when you tell her."

"Nah that's going to make it worst. She hasn't seen you since she caught us having sex in the house that day."

"Just see what she says. She might not beef."

"I'll see what she says, but she's probably gonna put me out." Beginning to cry again.

"Why are you crying?"

"Because I have no where to go."

"Just chill I will work everything out aight." Kissing her on the forehead.

"I gotta go home but I don't want to see this lady."

"If you want you can stay here but you gotta tell her eventually."

"You right. I'm just gonna see what she has to say."

"Call me and let me know what happens aight."

"You gonna walk me up the block."

"Don't I always big head."

"I'm just checking you might not want to mess with me since I'm pregnant."

"Shit you got my little man in you. Of course I'm gonna walk with you."

Smiling. "Who said we having a boy?"

"Yeah aight. My family only makes boys."

"Whatever. Pass me my coat."

"First give me a hug."

They stood in the middle of the bedroom and engaged in a passionate hug.

"Tanya you know I love you right?"

"Yeah and I love you too."

Chapter 12

Tony and Tanya walked in silence, hand in hand up Jersey Street in the hypothermic weather to confront Tanya's aunt. Their heart seemed to vibrate harder with each step they took towards meeting Dorothy. What seemed like the longest journey up Jersey Street finally came to an end. When they reached the house Tony noticed the worried look on Tanya's face.

"Tanya you aight?"

"Yeah I'm just trying to see how I'm gonna tell this lady."

"You want me to go in with you?"

"I told you that's going to make it worst. I'll be alright."

"Listen I'm going up to Ice's crib call me up there when yall finish talking aight."

"Alright."

"I love you."

"I love you too."

Tony walked off in the direction of Ice's house as Tanya put her key in the door to meet her match. When she entered the house everything was at ease. Dorothy was in her room with the door closed. Tanya figured she would be able to hold off her confession for another night, so she started getting ready for bed. When she turned her bedroom light off Dorothy's door screeched opened.

"Shit I know this lady is going to come fuck with me" Tanya thought to herself.

Dorothy walked into Tanya's room and flicked the light switch up.

"Where have you been?"

"I was at Me-Ka's house."

"You couldn't call and let me know where you was at?"

"I'm sorry."

"It's a quarter to eleven you been there since you got out of

school?"
"Yeah."
As she exited the room and walked towards the kitchen she spoke in a sarcastic tone. "I see you always find a way to wear out your welcome."

Tanya mumbled under her breath   "I'm tired of this lady."
She got out of the bed and met her aunt in the kitchen.
"Aunt Dorothy I have to talk to you about something."

Rolling her eyes. "If its not important I don't want to hear it right now."
Sighing, "Well its important."

Pouring a glass of Hawaiian Punch. "So speak."

Stammering over her words.   "I went to the doctor and they told me I'm pregnant."

Dorothy's blood began to boil as the shocked look on her face turned into disgust. Speaking in a hatred tone.
"I knew your little hot ass was pregnant when I didn't see you laying around the fucking house crying about cramps. But I gave you the benefit of the doubt, so I didn't say anything. Your gonna wined up just like your fucking mother."

"My mother ain't got nothing to do with this."
"Yes she does if she wasn't so fucking stupid, she wouldn't have got locked up and left you out here to fuck the world."
"What are you talking about I only had sex with one person."
"Yeah fucking right the streets talk."
"And they ain't saying nothing about me."
"No but they damn sure have a lot to say about your ace boon coon Me-Ka."
"And what does that have to do with me?"
"If she is out there fucking your out there doing the same damn thing."
"No I'm not Me-Ka is her own person."
"You know what you're so right. She may be fucking Tom,

Dick and Harry but she ain't stupid like your dumb ass to get pregnant."

Tears flowing down her face, Tanya walked out of the kitchen towards her room and slammed the door.
"I hope you went in there to pack your fucking bags. I already told your mother I ain't raising no more fucking kids that's not mines."

Tanya sat on the floor rocking back and forth in front of her full-length mirror wishing her mother wasn't incarcerated. She jumped at the sound of her aunt's bang at the door. She opened the door not knowing what to expect. Standing at the door was Dorothy with a box of hefty trash bags.

Handing Tanya the Box.
"I want all your shit out of my house by the time I come home from work tomorrow. Whatever is still here you can get it from off the curb." Walking away leaving Tanya standing there looking puzzled.

Stomach tightening up Tanya ran to the bathroom and began to throw up. Feeling dizzy and nauseous Tanya ran cold water on a wash cloth, sat down on the floor and placed it over her face.

"I'm not gonna make it through this shit." Tanya uttered with the little bit of energy she had left.

Following a few moments "I gotta get up."
Tanya managed to build up enough strength to make it out of the bathroom and onto her bed by sliding against the walls. She picked up the receiver to call Me-Ka but all she heard was,
"Hang up the fucking phone you hear me on it."

Tanya lay on the bed feeling faint blinking her eyes hoping she could stay awake.

Chapter 13

The next morning Tanya woke up to the nudge of Me-Ka's touch.

"Get up girl. You not going to school?"

Still in a dazed state "No I have to get up and start packing."

"What are you talking about? You still sleep?"

"No. That bitch kicked me out."

"You told your aunt?"

Getting out of the bed and walking towards the bathroom.

"Yeah and she told me to be out of her house by the time she gets home from work."

Following Tanya to the bathroom "Did you tell Tony?"

"I told him I was pregnant, but I didn't tell him I had to get out."

"So where are you going to stay?"

Talking with toothpaste in her mouth. "I don't know yet, but I do know where I won't be staying."

"Tanya you are lying. You are too calm for this to be true."

"I'm dead serious there ain't no reason to cry. She wants me out of her house so fuck her and I can't wait until I tell my mother this shit."

"I thought you and your aunt was cool."

Both of them walking out of the bathroom and into Tanya's room.

"We were. She's been acting like a bitch ever since she caught me and Tony having sex that day. So fuck her. I gotta call Tony and tell him what happened."

"Its 9 o'clock Tony is probably at school already."

"Damn you right."

They sat on the bed in silence until Me-Ka seen water filling up in Tanya's Eyes.
Wrapping her arm around Tanya's shoulder.
"Don't cry. You gonna have me in here crying with you."
"She knows I don't have anywhere to go and she's gonna to kick me out."
"Tanya stop worrying everything is gonna be aight."
Tears pouring down her face. "How? I don't have any family to call. My only family is in jail."

Tears dripping from her eyes.   "You know we are family. Let me ask my mother if you can stay with us."
"No. Your mother."
Cutting Tanya off. "Chill out. You know my mother sweats you."
Smiling, "You right. I need to talk to Tony though."

Standing up and wiping the tears from her eyes.
"I'm gonna walk up to school. See if I see Tony and then go holler at my mother before she goes to work."

Standing up to give Me-Ka a hug.
"Thank you."
"Don't sweat it that's what big sisters are for."
Both smiling
"Big sister. Yeah right."
"Aight. I'll be back in a minute."
"I'm gonna start putting my clothes in garbage bags before this lady comes home."

Me-Ka walked out of Tanya's room and out the front door thinking of a way to convince her mother of letting Tanya stay with them. As the door closed behind Me-Ka Tanya's phone rang. She was hesitant to answer it because she didn't want to hear her aunt beef anymore. But she hoped it would be Tony or her mother calling her.
"Hello."
"Why you didn't call me last night?"
"I tried but my fucking aunt was on the phone and I fell

asleep. "How did you know I was home?"

"You are always late. So what happened?"

"I told her and she kicked me out."

"Stop playing."

"I'm dead serious."

"She in the house now?"

"No."

"Aight. I'm about to come down there."

"Where you at?"

"I fell asleep at Ice crib waiting for you to call me last night."

"Me-ka just left here. She is on her way up to Curtis to look for you. Try to catch her before she gets all the way up there and your not there."

"Aight. I'll be there in a minute"

As Tanya hung up the phone she sighed in relief trusting that Tony would work everything out for her. While packing her clothes again her eyes filled up with tears as the thought of her father's death and mother's incarceration crossed her mind.

"Yo Ice I'm out."

"What happened now nigga?"

Tony grabbing his coat off of the pool table.

"Her aunt kicked her out after she told her she was pregnant."

"Damn kid where she at now?"

"She at the house now packing her shit."

Giving Tony a five.

"Yo Tone if she wants yall can stay here for a minute and I'll stay up stairs in my mom's crib."

"Aight good looking. Let me go check her out because she is crying all crazy. I'll holler at you later on."

"If I'm not here hit me on my cell."

"1"

Tony walked out the door and hastily walked to Tanya's house not remembering to look for Me-Ka. When Tanya opened the door Tony was shocked to see her face look stressed and hazel eyes so puffy.

"Hey."

"What up? You aight?"

"Yeah. Did you catch Me-Ka?"

"Yo I totally forgot. I came straight down here."

"Damn she probably half way up there now. I'm gonna call her on her cell phone."

"You should've did that in the first place."

"I know. I can't even think straight."

"You in here stressing yourself out. You seen your eyes?"

"What's wrong with my eyes?"

"Them shits look like you went 12 rounds with Muhammad Ali's daughter. Go look in the mirror."

Grabbing the cordless phone to call Me-Ka and walking to the bathroom to look in the mirror.

"You always got something to say."

Tanya returned to her bedroom where Tony was laying on the bed staring in space.

"Me-Ka said she is going to curse you out."

Sitting up motioning Tanya to sit on his lap   "I ain't scared. How far was she?"

"She was on Westervelt about to walk up the hill."

"Oh well."

"I don't know how I'm going to pack all these clothes."

"Ice said you can stay up there if you want and he will stay in his mom's crib."

"Me-Ka is about to ask her mother if I could stay with them for now. If her mother says no then I don't know where I'm gonna stay."

"Stop thinking negative."

Standing up off his lap and raising her voice.

"That's easy for you to say. You don't know what it feels like getting kicked out and not knowing where you're gonna stay."

"Relax yo. If her moms says you can stay there, stay there until I can get some bread to make something happen."

"Make what happen?"

"Just chill let me handle this."

Looking him dead in the eye   "Tony don't do nothing stupid."

Getting up off the bed and walking towards the door.

"I got this. Yo keep packing I'll be back in a minute. If Me-

Ka's mother says yes before I get back call Ice and let him know you need his truck to move your stuff."

"Where are you going?"

"I have to go talk to somebody. I'll be back" Walking out of the front door

Tanya had a feeling she shouldn't have let him leave the house but she didn't want to spark another argument between them so, she let him go.

CHAPTER 14

While walking up Jersey Street Tony's mind was running in shambles. He understood it was his responsibility to take care of the love of his life that was nourishing his unborn child. Tony knew he was going to step to the plate but he didn't have any bread stacked to handle that responsibility. His only alternative was to play the urban hustle (the drug game). While walking he thought about the three people he knew that could put him on.

"I can ask Ice but that nigga is gonna give me a song and dance. I could still fuck with the nigga Money B or Knowledge. The nigga Knowledge probably ain't gonna try to here me either. Fuck it I'm just gonna call Knowledge and see what he's talking about."

He stopped at the pay phone on Jersey Street across the street from the shoemaker to call Knowledge.

"Peace."
"Knowledge what up?"
"Who this?"
"Tony."
"Little Tony?"
"Yeah."
"Oh what up God?"
"I'm chilling. Yo I need to holler at you about something."
"Go ahead. What up?"
"Nah I can't speak on this phone."
"Where you at right now?"
"I'm on a pay phone on Jersey Street."
"Aight I'm dropping my girl off at the ferry. I'll be over there in a minute."
"I'm in front of the shoemaker."
"I'll be there in like ten minutes. Everything aight though?"

"I'm gonna kick it with you when I see you."
"Aight I'm on my way."
"1."

Tony hung up the phone with a smile. He was excited because he thought his dilemma would be handled.

Me-Ka sprinted up Jersey Street like she was running the hundred-Yard-dash, to tell Tanya they could be roommates. Me-Ka entered Tanya's house and found her sitting on the edge of her bed day-dreaming.

"Tanya, Tanya..."
"Oh. Hey."
"I know you heard me calling you."
"How long was you calling me?"
"Stop playing. You aight?"
"Yeah I'm aight. This shit is killing me though."
"You don't have to stress yourself out no more. My moms said you can come stay with us."
"Are you sure?"
"I wouldn't have ran up the block and be out of breath if she said no."
Standing up to give Me-Ka a hug. "Thank you so much."
"I told you already that's what big sisters are for."
"Me-Ka thank you."
"Cut that mushy shit out lets pack your clothes up before your aunt comes home."
"Yeah you right. I damn sure don't want to see her ass."

As they packed Tanya's belongings Me-ka reminisced about places where Tanya wore particular outfits to keep her mind off her pre-dicament.

"Yo how are we gonna get all these clothes down to my house?"
"Oh that's right. Tony said you had to call Ice for his truck."
"I know Tony didn't say no shit like that."
Smiling, "Yes he did."

With a serious tone "Tony knows damn well I haven't spoke to Ice since he tried to videotape me."

"I'm telling you Tony told me to tell you to call him."
"Well there is a change of plans. You're gonna call up there and ask him."
Smiling, "You hold grudges for real. Pass me the phone."
Passing Tanya the phone, "Where is Tony anyway? We're gonna need his help moving your stuff."

Dialing Ice's number "He was here for like ten or fifteen minutes I told him what happened and he said he'll be back. He told me he had to go handle something."

"Don't tell that mother fucker I'm here either."
"Stop fronting. You know you miss him."
"Please."
"He ain't answering. What's his cell number?"
"1-917-442-9797"
"I knew you were still feeling him."
Smirking   "Because I memorized his number?"
"That's right people I hate I don't know their number."
"Whatever."
Ringing Ice's phone. "What the fuck ever then."

"Peace who this?"
"Tanya."
"Oh what up Tanya? You aight?"
"I had better days, but I'll be aight."
"True. You're a soldier."
"You ain't never lie."
Laughing "You looking for Tony?"
"Is he with you?"
"Nah he left my house earlier he said he was going to check you."
"Oh yeah he came to my house earlier than left. I was really calling because he told me to ask you if I could hold your truck to move my stuff to Me-Ka's house."
"You need it right now?"
"No in like a hour if that's good."
"Yeah. I'll bring it to your house in like forty-five minutes."

"Thank you so much Ice."

"Yo you know how to drive?"

"No. Hopefully Tony will be back if not Me-ka knows how to drive." Chuckling.

"You a funny girl."

"She right here you want to talk to her?"

"Yeah put her on the phone."

"Hold on."

Tanya with a grin on her face turned away from Me-Ka and handed her the phone.

Reaching for the phone, "You play too much."

"You know you want to talk to him."

"Hello."

"Yo what up?"

Nonchalantly, "Hi Spike Lee."

"Why you call me that?"

"Because you like filming people."

"There you go. I told you the camera wasn't on."

"So you say."

"Aight. So when I drop the car off you gonna speak to me?"

"I'll listen to what you have to say."

"Aight then I'll see you later."

"Bye."

"You are so stank."

"You shouldn't have gave me the phone."

"You know damn well you wanted to hear his voice."

"He wanted to hear my voice."

"Oh I started her conceited ass up."

CHAPTER 15

Tony waited impatiently for Knowledge in front of the shoe-maker watching people walk in and out the store playing lotto. The thought of being a stick up kid crossed his mind, but deep down inside he knew he wasn't built for it. As Knowledge pulled up Tony's heart started beating fast he didn't know what to expect. He got in the car and they drove off.

"What up Knowledge?"
"Shit I'm chilling. Take a ride with me."
"Yeah."
"Yo why you not in school?"
"I gotta handle something."
"What you got a problem with somebody?"
"Nah it ain't nothing like that, but I do need your help"
"Spit."
"I gotta make some quick paper."
"What you need paper for?"
"My girl is pregnant and her aunt kicked her out. Its only right I step up."
"Where her moms and pops at?"
"Remember the dude that them blood niggas killed in the stair case down the block."
"That was her pops?"
"Yeah and her moms is locked up."
Lighting up a blunt, "Her moms is locked up? You trying to smoke?"
"Nah I'm good. Yeah she was locked up before her pops died."
"Damn shorty is living a rough life."
"That's why I'm telling you I have to step up."
"Her aunt kicked her out, so where she staying?"
"She probably gonna stay with her friend and her moms. If

not Ice said she can stay at his crib."
"That's some bullshit her aunt did."
"Who you telling?"

Blowing smoke out of the window "Aight so what's your plan?"
"I need you to put me on."
"Son we already had this conversation about hustling."
"God I know but right now that's my only option."
"Nah you know I can't do that."
"Knowledge I'm asking you to do me this one favor and you're shitting on me. Every time I see you, you always say if I need something to holler at you. Now I'm hollering."
"Yo Tone I can't have that shit on my conscious if something happens to you out here. These niggas out here are playing for keeps."

Raising his voice "Right now you think I give a fuck about these niggas out here."
"God I know you want to look out for your girl and all and I respect that, but this drug shit ain't for you that shit ain't for me. You don't know half of the shit I go through everyday just to survive kid."
"Look you said it yourself the hustling shit ain't for you but you getting by right? You're making it happen in these streets. Niggas respect you out here."
"Yeah and that respect didn't come from hustling. That shit came from dealing with motherfuckers that was out of line. I got shit on my resume that I regret to this day. And my word is bond you ain't ready for this shit and I'm not gonna expose you to it either."
"Yo I respect what you're saying, but I gotta get some bread. Niggas in the streets clowning me that I work at the movies that's weak"
"Fuck it do what you do. Those same niggas clowning you in ten years they are still gonna be walking up and down Jersey Street clowning people. The same niggas that was clowning me in West Brighton when I was younger those are the same niggas that's making me rich. My workers sell crack to them every fucking day"
"I feel what your saying but me working at the movies ain't gonna get me that real paper."
"God trust me if I could go back and know that shit I know now I would do exactly what you're doing. This shit I'm doing ain't worth it. You think I'm hitting you with the bullshit because I don't want to

put you on, but listen to me kid I seen all this shit."

Knowledge made a U-turn and they rode in silence down Jersey Street.

"Yo where you want me to drop you off at?"
"Drop me off at my girls crib at the corner of Hendricks."
They continued their mute ride down the street until Knowledge parked the car at the bus stop across the street from Tanya's crib. Knowledge reached in his pocket, pulled out a roll of money and handed Tony five hundred-dollar bills.
"Here take this aight."
"Good looking."
"It ain't about nothing. Just remember what I said."
"Aight."
Tony got out the car and closed the door. Knowledge drove off and beeped the horn as Tony walked across the street to Tanya's house.

Chapter 16

"Hey sweetie where you coming from?"

"I had to holler at my man."

"Who's your man?"

"Why? Just chill out."

"Tony you got your period?"

"Whatever what did Me-Ka's mother say?"

"She said I could stay there. Me-Ka is in my room now helping me pack."

"Did you call Ice for the truck?"

"He said he's gonna bring it by in an hour. Tony what is wrong with you? You look like you're up to something."

Sucking his teeth. "Damn leave it alone."

"Can you help me finish packing?"

"How much more you got?"

"We emptied out my two dressers. I still got all those clothes in the closet and my shoes that's in the hallway closet."

"Tanya you taking all those fucking shoes?"

"Yes. My aunt said she's gonna throw away whatever I don't take."

"You don't need all those damn shoes. I'm not carrying them either."

"Did I ask you to carry anything?"

"Keep getting fucking smart and you'll move all this shit by yourself."

Walking out of the living room "If not helping me is gonna make you feel like a man than don't help."

Tony sat on the sofa and thought about the sex episode he and Tanya shared on that sofa. "I turned this shit into semen furniture." As his imagination was flowing he was interrupted by Me-Ka walking into the room. Before Me-Ka could speak Tony's imagination really started running wild the thoughts he had of Tanya turned into thoughts of Me-Ka.

"Why you got a smile on your face?"

Smiling   "If you only knew."

"Yeah aight. Are you gonna help us pack her stuff up?"

"She told you to ask me that? She pops all that shit then sends you in here."

"No. Are you gonna help us or what?"

"I know you lying but I'll be in there in a minute."

"Hurry up."

"See now I'm gonna take longer."

Tony watched as Me-Ka's butt switched from side to side in a perfect-motion as she strolled back to the room. Tony didn't walk in the room behind Me-ka because he didn't want his girl to see his man standing at attention. After Tony got himself under control he walked to Tanya's room and began emptying her closet into garbage bags.

When Ice parked his truck in front of Tanya's house Money B was driving down the opposite side of the street. Ice beeped the horn to say what up but when Money B realized it was Ice he pulled over and got out of his car.

"He's gonna try to talk my ear off. I should've never beeped the fucking horn" Ice spoke to himself.

Ice got out the car and greeted Money B.

"What up nigga?"

"Shit I'm chilling. I didn't recognize the truck. When you got the windows tinted?"

"Just now."

"At night the truck is gonna look crazy."

"Yeah I know."

"All you need now is some rims."

"I ordered them Sprewell spinning joints."

"So you really getting money out here huh?"

"Nah it ain't no money out here."

"Yeah aight nigga. It ain't everyday a nigga from the hood order some spinners."

"I got lucky."

"Yo what you doing over here?"

"I'm letting Tony hold the truck so he can move his girl shit down the block."

"What she moving?"

"Yeah her and her aunt beefing."

"Where she moving to?"

"She moving to Me-Ka's crib, but you a nosey nigga."

"Whatever I was just talking but I'm about to be out you need a ride somewhere?"

"Nah I'm straight."

"Aight one."

"Chill out."

Money B walked off to his car. Ice sat on the red pole in front of Tanya's crib and dialed Me-Ka's cell phone.

"Hello."

"Yo I'm outside."

"Why you didn't knock on the door?"

"I didn't know if her aunt was in there."

"Bye. I'm about to open the door."

Me-Ka opened the door and was upset to see Ice still sitting on the pole.

"Didn't I just tell you I was opening the door?"

"And."

"So why you still sitting on the pole?"

Standing up off the pole and walking to the door.

"I'm supposed to run to the door?"

Moving back to let him in the house.

"I see you didn't change none. You still doing stupid shit."

"You didn't change none either. You still got that stink ass attitude."

"But you wish this stank ass attitude was in your life."

Laughing "You are so conceited."

"That's what you like about me."

Smiling, "That's not all I like."

Walking towards Tanya's bedroom.
"Too bad all you can have is my attitude."

They entered Tanya's bedroom and Ice spoke.
"Oh shit Tony I didn't know you was here."
"I got here a minute ago."
Giving each other a five.
"Hey Tanya how you feeling?"
"I'm good."
"Damn what you doing with all these clothes?"
Smiling "This ain't a lot."
"You can open up a Macys in this motherfucker."
"You crazy Ice."

Passing Tony the keys to his truck.
"Yo here goes the keys I parked in the front."
"Good looking."

Me-Ka spoke up.
"We could've used your help. But I know you're too pretty to help."
Sighing "There you go. Nah I gotta go handle something."

"Ice don't pay her no mind. Thank you for letting me hold your truck."
"Tanya I ain't worried about her."
"What time you need the truck back?"
"Whenever yall finish."
"Thank you."
"Just do me one favor make sure you don't roll down the windows, I just got them tinted."
"Alright we won't."
"Aight I'll see yall later. Yo Tony hit me on my cell when yall finish."
"Aight."

"Thanks again Ice." Tanya screamed as he walked out the door.
"Don't sweat it."

CHAPTER 17

Knowledge sat in front of Ice's house waiting for his return thinking about the conversation he had with Tony's older brother. The night Tony's brother laid on his deathbed dying from a gunshot wound wasn't meant for him. He gave his best friend his word that he would look out for his younger brother. Knowledge wanted to holler at Ice and make sure Tony didn't have any options into the drug game.

When Ice got to the corner of his block he spotted Knowledge's car. He didn't know what to expect so he reached in his waistline and confirmed his beretta wasn't on safety. Knowledge laughed as he watched Ice's every move through his rear view mirror. When Ice got two cars behind him Knowledge beeped the horn and signaled his hand for Ice to come to the car. He approached the car with fear and talked to Knowledge through the passenger side window.

"What up?"

"I gotta holler at you. Get in."

Ice was shook as he got in the car. "What happened?"

"Nothing happened. I need you to do me a favor."

"What?"

"First off little nigga relax I'm not gonna do nothing to you and that shit you did back there could've got you killed."

"What?"

Nonchalantly "I seen you reach for your gun when you saw my car. If some niggas was coming to stick you, you already let them know you had a gun. They would've got out the car blazing. You wouldn't have had a chance. Use your head. Anyway did Tony ask you to set him out?"

Nervously, "Nah why you say that?"

"He hollered at me and asked me to put him on. He said he needed some paper for his girl."

"He told me about his girl getting kicked out but he didn't

say nothing about hustling."

"I know if he asked me he's definitely gonna get at you. If he gets at you do me that favor and dead him."

"Yeah. Tony know I'm not gonna put him on that's probably why he didn't ask me."

"Yo I need you to give me your word with that."

"My word is bond."

"Aight. I'm gone but don't even mention it to him that we had this conversation and nigga be smarter with your gun."

Smiling and wiping his sweaty palm on his jeans before he gave Knowledge a five, "Aight. Chill out."

Ice got out the car, Knowledge drove off shaking his head and thinking to himself.

"These wannabe gangsters."

As they finished emptying Tanya's closet into garbage bags.

"Yo what else needs to be done?"

"Just my shoes in the hallway closet but me and Me-Ka can do that. Can you start bringing the bags to the car?"

"Yeah, but you know we are gonna have to take more than one trip."

"Tony if you lay down the seats in the truck we should only have to make two trips."

"Hell no we're gonna have to make a trip with just your shoes."

"Damn we gotta hurry up its almost 2:30 and Dorothy gets off of work at 5:00 today."

Tony took off his white T-shirt, wearing a wife beater and began carrying Tanya's department store to Ice's truck. Me-Ka took notice to Tony's frame while Tanya was out the room and spoke to herself

"He can get it". When Tanya returned to the room Me-Ka spoke up.

"Tanya you got lucky with Tony."

"Why you say that?"

"He's a good dude. The rest of these New Brighton niggas would be no where to be found right now."

"Some of them would be there but the rest ha."

"You really got lucky because he's cute and he's a good dude."

"You ain't never lie. My baby is fly."

"Usually the ugly ones are the nice guys."

"That's because their ugly asses don't have a choice but to be nice."

"You better not lose him. These bitches will grab him up in a minute."

As Tony walked back in the room   "He ain't going no where."

"Who ain't going no where?"

Me-Ka spoke up, "There you go minding our business."

"Yall in here talking about other niggas I'm telling Ice."

"Please ain't nobody scared or worried about Ice."

"Hey baby she was in heaven earlier when I let her speak to him on the phone."

"I know. She's acting for TV. She knows damn well that she misses my man. We know she's gonna give him a second chance she needs to stop fronting."

"Please your man wishes I gave him a second chance."

"Whatever. Yo I can't fit nothing else in the truck."

"Aight so lets leave this and make the first trip."

"Yo I folded down the back seat so only one of yall can come unless yall sit on each others lap in the front."

"Nah you and Me-Ka go so she can show you where to put the stuff and I can finish packing before you make the next trip."

"Aight come on little Ice."

Tony and Me-Ka rode to her house and unpacked Tanya's belongings laughing and joking up until they brought the last garbage bag into Me-Ka's room. Tony had trouble bringing the bag into the room due to fatigue.

"You walking around with a wife beater on and you can't carry that little ass bag."

"Shit I still look good in this wife beater."

"I don't know why you got it on, your little ass and beating nobody."

Flirtatiously "I may be little but I make up for it in other places."

Biting her bottom lip and glancing at the zipper area in his jeans.

"So I heard."

Tony surprised by her response walked pass Me-Ka and bumped into her. Me-Ka desiring his touch grabbed Tony from the back and threw him on the bed.

"I knew your little ass was weak."

Tony got up off the bed and wrapped his arms around Me-Ka to slam her on the bed. As he went to slam her she wrapped her arms around him and they fell on the bed together with Tony on top of her. For a split second the thought of kissing her crossed his mind but he didn't want to play himself. Me-Ka stared into his eyes waiting for him to make a move but he refused.

As he got up "Yo we gotta get the rest of the stuff."

Furious he refused, "Yeah you right."

They rode in the elevator and back to Tanya's house in silence both wondering if the other one would tell Tanya. When they reached her house they both acted as if everything was normal. As they walked in the house Tanya was finishing up emptying her shoes out of the closet.

"Yall back already?"

"How long you thought it was going to take?"

"Tony you always got something smart to say."

"Shut up. You ready to make the next trip."

"I'm going on this one?"

"Yeah what you thought we was going to do all the work.

"See Me-Ka I told you she was gonna get lazy."

"You damn sure did say that. Bring your lazy ass on."

"You going too Me-Ka?"

"Yeah so we can get it done faster."

"Aight let me put some sneakers on. Start bringing the bags to the car."

"Hurry up too and don't try to take your time so you don't have to bring bags to the car."

"Shut up Me-Ka you think you know everything."

"I don't know everything but I know your ugly ass."

"Ill. Just bring the bags to the car."

They packed her things into the truck and transported them to Me-Ka's house. Two of them at a time brought the clothes to Me-Ka's apartment in the elevated while the other person bought the bags from the truck to the elevator. On one of Tanya's trips from the car to the elevated she heard a voice behind her say.

"You're too fly to be doing all that work."
Turning around and smiling. "Thank you."

"Can I stop you for a minute?"
Stopping, Sighing and rolling her eyes in the air.

"You have thirty seconds."

Smiling "Do you remember my name?"

"Money B right?"

"Yeah. Did your friend give you my number?"

"Yeah."

"What you threw it away or something?"

"No. I still have it."

"Why have it if your not gonna use it?"

"I was being nice. I can throw it away if you want."

"Nah. Are you gonna use it?"

"I have a man."

"Listen just hold on to the number if you're ever lonely or if you need something use it aight."

"We'll see but I have to get back to moving my stuff."

"You need some help?"

"No. My man is enough help."

"Aight. Shorty but don't work too hard."

Money B watched as Tanya switched her way into the building and thought to himself.

"Some way or another I'm gonna get shorty."

Chapter 18

Ice lay on his bed trying to rest off the stress of his lifestyle. When he heard a knock at the door. He got out the bed frustrated, reached under his pillow and put his tool back in his waistline.

"A nigga can never get a break."

He peeked out the window and seen a dude standing with his back to the door. He didn't recognize the dude's shape so he stared out the window until Dramah turned towards the door to knock again. Opening the door

"Oh shit it's the God."

"You busy right now?"

"Nah I was trying to lay down for a minute. Come in God."

"What you just had some chick in here or something?"

"Nah. I don't be getting no-sleep. Every time I lay down my phone ring. I gotta drop this off I gotta pick this up. This shit is gonna drive me crazy."

Sitting down on Ice's sofa.

"You better get some soldiers."

"Nah you can't trust these niggas no more God. You never know whose smoking now. I'll fuck around and have to kill one of these dudes."

"Damn. Shit wasn't like that when I was getting it."

"Word. What up though? You still in the gym?"

"Yeah. I got my first fight in two weeks in Jersey."

"Word already? That's good."

"When I seen you in the Wave I told you I still had it. God when I was up North I was training everyday."

"Don't get out to Jersey and get your wig pushed back."

"Never. You know me better than that."

"Aight. Yo what you doing out here?"

"You know my peoples live down the block. I was in front of their crib and Money B rode by. I knew you laid your head on the block but I didn't remember the house. He pointed your crib out to me."

"Yeah I seen his nosey ass on Jersey Street earlier."

"He told me you just got your windows tinted or something like that."

"Yeah."

Standing up off the couch.

"But yo I ain't trying to hold you up let me get back down to my people's crib."

"No question. Yo let me know when the fight is I'll drive out to Jersey to check you nah mean."

Walking towards the door.

"Yeah I'll let you know."

"You good though, you need something?"

Giving Ice a five

"Nah I'm straight. Good looking."

Ice closed the door and walked towards his bed when the phone rang.

"This shit don't ever end."

"Hello."

"You still handling what was so important?"

"You called to bother me or you called to speak to me?"

"You don't deserve me calling you at all but I was bored."

"How are you bored I thought you was helping Tone and Tanya move her stuff?"

"I am but they went up the block to get the rest of her stuff."

"And you thought about me how sweet."

"Don't flatter yourself."

"You ain't call me in like a month. You up to something."

"I ain't up to nothing. I told you I called because I was bored."

"So I guess you ain't mad at me no more."

"I didn't say all that. You have a lot of making up to do."

"Oh so now I can have more than just your stank attitude?"

"If you act right."

"So when can I see you to act right?"

"You tell me you're the busy one."

"I have an open schedule."

"Aight so I'll call you tonight after I finish helping Tanya

unpack. It might be late so tell your chicks to be easy."
"There you go. 1."

Ice hung up the phone with a smile on his face.
"She must be backed up or something."

As Tony and Tanya pulled up in front of her house to load the truck
Dorothy was closing the front door.
"I thought you said she got off at five o'clock today?"
"She was supposed to. She probably left early to see what
I was doing."
"Fuck it go in there and bring your shoes to the door and I'll
put them in the truck."
"I know she's gonna try to start a argument."
"Don't say nothing to her just get your shit and be out."
"It's not that easy with her."
"Just go ahead."
Tanya got out of the truck, put her key in the door and tried to open
it but the chain stopped her from entering. Dorothy came to the
door and spoke to her with the chain still on the door.
"I thought I told you to have your shit out before I got home."
"I was but you came home early."
"Oh well."
"Can you please open the door so I can get the rest of my
stuff?"
Raising her voice.
"I told you to have your shit out."
Tanya sucked her teeth.
"You making a scene for no reason."
"I don't give a fuck. That's why you pregnant now your little
fast ass think you can do whatever you want."
"What you talking about? What does you having the chain
on the door have to do with me being pregnant? You make
no sense."

Tony got out of the truck and walked towards the door.
"Tanya forget it just get in the car."
"No I want the rest of my stuff."
"She ain't gonna let you in the house. You're gonna be out
here screaming for no reason."

Taking the chain off the door.

"You know what hurry up, get your shit and get the fuck out of my house."

"That's what I was trying to do from the beginning."

"And his little disrespectful ass better not come in my house."

Tanya managed to get the rest of her things into the truck without arguing with her aunt. She and Tony brought her belongings into the building and took turns walking them up the steps because the elevator was broke. When they finally finished all three of them laid on Me-Ka's bed exhausted.

"Yall gonna unpack all this stuff tonight?"

"I'm gonna try to get most of it done."

"Yo let me bring Ice his truck."

"Aight thanks for your help baby. Tell Ice I said thank you again."

"Call me at my house if you need me later on."

"Aight. I love you."

"I love you too. Later Me-Ka."

"Bye Tony."

Tony walked out the door.

"Yall are perfect for each other."

"Why you say that?"

"Listen to yall. I love you, I love you too."

"Stop hating."

"I ain't hating that's cute. I told you earlier don't lose him. One of these bitches will definitely grab him up."

Chapter 19

Tony walked out of the building again thinking about how he could get his hands on some bread to get them an apartment. As he drove to the corner of Richmond Terrace and Jersey Street he spotted Money B's car parked in front of the twenty-four-hour store.

"This nigga gotta be in the store."

Tony made a left turn on York Avenue and waited to see if Money B would walk out of the store. He sat for a minute but was anxious so he got out the car and walked in the store. Tony greeted Money B at the counter waiting for a beef pattie.

"What up?"

"Shit what up with you?"

"On the real I gotta holler at you."

"About what?"

"I'm gonna kick it with you when you finish in here."

"Aight."

Money B figured he wanted to holler at him about Tanya. As he waited for his beef pattie he watched Tony's every move in front of the store because he left his burner in the car. When he finished in the store he got up close on Tony just in case he had to wrestle him.

"So what up?"

"Your offer still good?"

"What offer?"

"The offer you made me in Ice's crib yesterday."

"God I don't know what you're talking about."

"You said if I wanted a bomb to come holler at you."

"Oh so you're tired of smelling like popcorn and butter?"

"Whatever. Are you gonna hit me or not?"

"I thought you was good what made you wanna step your game up?"

"I gotta get some paper. My girl and her peoples are beefing I'm trying to get us an apartment."

"I feel you."

"Stop playing are you gonna hit me with the work?"

"Nah. Money B thought for a minute and changed his answer."

"Matter of fact I got you. Come check me tonight at like 11-11:30 in Stapelton."

"Where?"

"218 Broad Street Apartment 3c."

"Good looking."

They departed their separate ways. Tony thought Money B had his best interest at hand but he really had an ulterior motive.

Tony drove to Ice's crib excited while Money B made a phone call.

"Detective Patrick speaking."

"I got something for you."

"What is it?"

"Some dude is gonna be moving major weight tonight in Stapelton."

"When and where?"

"Just be behind 218 Broad Street at a quarter to twelve."

"How I know this ain't some bullshit?"

"Did I ever give you bullshit?"

"Alright who am I looking for?"

"After he makes his move I will call you. Just be behind 218."

"How much I owe you for this one?"

"I don't want nothing from you, whatever you find on him I want."

"Done deal. Don't fuck me on this one."

Tony parked the truck in front of Ice's crib and beeped the horn. He got out the car and knocked on the door just as Ice started his first dream.

"I can't buy a fucking nap."

Ice got out the bed and opened the door for Tony.

"Yall niggas are gonna stop coming here when I'm trying to sleep."

"Stop crying."

"Yall finished moving already?"

"Yeah a little while ago."

"So you ready to be a daddy?"

"Hell no but I can't do shit about it now."

"Yes you can."

"What?"

"Tell her to get an abortion."

"Nah. She already said she don't believe in them so I didn't even bring it up. You know I was thinking that from the beginning."

"Guess who called me?"

"Tanya already told me she gave Me-Ka the phone."

"Nah she called me again when you and your girl went to move the stuff."

"Word. She was fronting then. Talking all that shit. Your man wishes I gave him a second chance."

"Yeah you know she is thirsty for the kid."

"She seen the tints and she was like yeah I gotta keep him."

"Nah she's backed up. She seen me earlier and was like yeah I gotta get him back."

"Whatever, you think you that nigga?"

"Yeah it's hard being me."

"Watch she's gonna play hard to get. She ain't gonna give you none for a minute."

"You crazy I'm gonna take her to 42nd tonight make her feel important than smash."

"Yeah aight. It sounds good."

"I'm gonna call you as soon as I smash."

"What time yall going?"

"She said she's gonna call me when they finish unpacking Tanya's stuff."

"Shit they gonna be in there all day."

"Yo how big is her room?"

"It's big but they both got mad clothes."

"Oh yeah they gonna be beefing."

"Yeah I said that to myself earlier. That's why I gotta try to get some paper to get us an apartment."

"I told you if you need something to get at me."

Reaching to give Ice a five.

"Nah I'm straight right now. But yo let me go lay down I'm tired as fuck from moving all her shit."

"Word. That's what I was trying to do before your bitch ass

woke me up."

Walking towards the door.

"Nigga you just lazy. Where you want me to put your keys before I forget?"

"Put them shits by the door and put the lock on the door behind you."

"Aight. Yo hit me before you go to forty-deuce. 1000"

"1."

Chapter 20

Tanya and Me-Ka had small talk as they began unpacking Tanya's belongings.

"I spoke to Ice again."

"After you spoke to him at my aunt's house?"

"Yeah I called him when you and Tony made that last trip."

"So yall cool again?"

"I mean I'm supposed to get up with him tonight but it ain't gonna be what it used too be."

"Whatever. You know damn well once he starts feeling up on you, you ain't gonna know what to do with yourself."

"Please I can control myself."

"You can control yourself but you can't control your hormones."

"Shit Ice was the last person I fucked and that was almost two months ago anything can happen tonight."

"You a clown. Oh yeah I seen your peoples today."

"Who?"

Blushing.

"Money B."

"Where did you see him?"

"In front of the building when I was bringing the stuff in."

"You was with Tony wasn't you?"

"Nah Tony had already went up stairs."

"You talked to him?"

"Yeah. He seems cool."

Shaking her head.

"You playing with fire."

"How you figure?"

"When Tony catch you talking to him I'm gonna be planning your funeral."

"I know how to handle Tony."

"Yeah aight. What was yall talking about anyway?"

"See you talking about I'm playing with fire but your ass wanna know what we was talking about."

"You know you was gonna tell me anyway."

Shrugging her shoulders.

"Nah he asked me if I still had his number. And he just said if I'm lonely or if I need something to holler at him. Real brief."

"You still got his number?"

"I put it in my wallet that day. I think it's still in there."

"Oh yeah you like him."

"I said he seems cool."

"I thought you was happy with Tony?"

"I am. I just need some excitement in my life."

"You got a good dude."

"Don't get me wrong I love Tony but right now with my aunt and everything I need something new that's gonna stop me from worrying."

"All I can tell you is make sure you make the right choice."

"You right. I'm not gonna dis Tony he's always gonna be my baby."

At 10:00 Tony laid in his bed thinking about getting caught up in the drug game. Knowledge's words and the death of his brother gave him doubts. The thought of his love for Tanya made him feel obligated to provide for her and his unborn child. Tony got out the bed put on an Akademiks sweat suit with a fresh pair of white uptowns and a Yankees fitted.

"Fuck it I gotta do what I gotta do."

Tony walked into the kitchen and was greeted by his mother.

"What up ma?"

"I told you about talking to me like I'm one of those chicks in the street."

"Aight ma."

"You about to go out?"

"Yeah for a little while. I left my report card on your bed yesterday."

"I seen it I'm so proud of you sweetheart."

"Thanks."

"What time you think you're gonna be home?"

"I'm gonna be at Ice's house so whenever I get tired."

"Alright just be careful out there."
Giving his mother a hug and a kiss on the cheek.
"I will."
"I love you."
"I love you too ma."
Tony grabbed his coat off the living room chair and walked out into the concrete jungle. Tony stood in front of his house and contemplated where the nearest pay phone was. He walked to the store on Westervelt Avenue and called a cab to Stapelton. Tony lingered in front of the store convinced he could handle what he was about to get himself into. The cab came right away and he was off to get his bomb from Money B. He got out the cab in the back of Money B's building and walked through the under path into the building. The elevator was taking forever so he took the steps up to the third floor and knocked on 3c. A dude he never seen before answered the door looking grimy.
"Peace is Money B here?"
"What's your name?"
"Tony."
"Yo he's not here but he left a pack for you. Hold up."
He left Tony at the door and returned with a black book bag."
"Yo there is a half of an ounce in here. He said he will
check you in three days to get his bread."
Grabbing the bag from the dude.
"Aight good looking."

Tony walked to the elevator with regrets of taking the bomb from Money B but it was too late.

Money B sat in his bedroom and made his phone call as soon as Tony walked away from his door.

"Detective Patrick speaking."
"Yo he's about to walk out the building."
"What is he wearing?"
"Hold on let me ask my man. Yo what the nigga got on?"
"A black coat with some blue sweat pants and a Yankee
fitted."
"Hello. Yeah he got on a black coat, blue sweat pants, a
hat and a black book bag."

"Alright we see him."
"When am I gonna get what we talked about?"
"I will call you tomorrow so we can meet up."
"Aight."
"Thanks for your help I owe you one."

Money B hung up the phone with a smile on his face. Detective
Patrick spoke to his crew over the air.

"Listen up that's the kid that just got out the cab. He's
probably going to walk up to the cab station on the corner.
Keep an eye on him. If he gets in a cab stay behind the
cab for two blocks than do a routine check. Let's do this
efficient and everybody be safe."

Tony did exactly what the detective said; he walked to New Port
cab station on the corner of Broad Street and Tompkins Avenue.
When he got to the station there was a vacant cab waiting. He got
in the front seat and they drove in the direction of New Brighton.

An unmarked car followed them until they reached the
Stapelton Library then pulled them over. When Tony heard the
sirens and seen the red lights flashing his heart jumped into the
back seat. The cops were at the passenger door so fast Tony
didn't have a chance to stash the half of ounce.

Tony's dreams vanished when the officer asked him to step
out of the car. There was no reason to try talking his way out of the
arrest when the detective pulled his bomb out of the book bag.
The detectives read him his rights and transported him to the 120
pct.

Tears strolled down Tony's face as he sat handcuffed to a
chair waiting for his phone call. After he was fingerprinted and took
his mug shot he was granted his phone call. Although he didn't
want to he had the detective call his mother.

"Hello."
"May I speak to Mrs. Clark please?"
"Speaking."
"This is detective Patrick from the 120 pct. I have your son
Anthony here with me."
"Oh my God. What happened?"
"We were doing a routine check and we found a good
amount of drugs on him."

"Drugs?"

"Yes. Tomorrow morning in criminal court he will be charged with possession of an illegal substance with the intent to sell. I have him right here next to me would you like to speak with him?"

"Yes."

Detective Patrick handed Tony the phone with a smirk.

"Hello."

"Anthony what are you doing with drugs?"

"I didn't know there was drugs in the bag."

"In what bag?"

"The bag they found it in."

"Whose bag was it?"

"Ma I gotta go but please come to court tomorrow. It's on Targee Street."

"What time?"

"9:00. I love you ma."

"I love you too Anthony."

Tears began to pour out of her eyes. Mrs. Clark sat on her bed with the phone to her ear in a daze. After a while she hung up the phone, laid on her bed and looked at a portrait of her two sons. One deceased and the other one now in a holding cell.

CHAPTER 21

The telephone rang and Mrs. Clark jumped up thinking it would be Tony calling again.

"Hello."

"Good evening Mrs. Clark this is Ice is Tony home?"

"Ice could you come by my house? I need to speak with you."

Hearing the seriousness in her voice.

"Is everything alright?"

"No that's why I really need to talk with you."

"Alright I'm leaving my house now I'll be there in five minutes."

"Thank you Ice. I'll see you when you get here."

"Bye."

Ice hung up the phone confused to what was going on ran out his house, jumped in his car and sped his way to Tony's crib. When he reached the house Tony's mother was at the front door waiting for him. He knew something had happened as soon as he looked her in face and seen her eyes were bloodshot red from crying.

"Thank you for coming Ice."

"No problem what happened?"

"Come inside first."

They walked in the house and they both sat on the love seat sofa in the living room.

"Ice I received a phone call a little while ago from the 120 pct."

"Ok."

"They have Anthony."

"For what?"

"The detective said they found a good amount of drugs on him."

"No way. Tony don't mess with drugs he's scared to take advil."

"I know. They said he had the intent to sell."

"Mrs. Clark Tony does not sell drugs. He goes to school
and works everyday. I know for a fact he doesn't sell drugs."

"Ice you are a respectful kid that's why I never had a problem with you coming to my home or Anthony being at your
mother's home. Now I have heard from a few people that
you are involved with drugs. I never judged you because I
don't have a heaven or a hell to put you in but I need you to
tell me the truth was Anthony selling drugs with you?

"Tony never got involved with me. He was always telling me
to stop that's how I know for a fact he wasn't selling drugs."

"When Anthony left the house earlier he said he was going
to your house. Did he take a bag from your house that
could've had drugs in it?"

"Mrs. Clark I haven't seen Tony since earlier when he left
my house and said he was going home to go to sleep. I
was supposed to go on a date that's why I was calling to
see if he wanted to bring Tanya."

"Ok do you know anyone else's house he goes to where he
could've picked up a bag with drugs?"

"Not off the top of my head. We don't hangout with other
people it has always been me and Tony. The only other
house he could've went to was Tanya's house."

"No one in her house deals with drugs right?"

"She just moved in with one of her friends down the block in
the projects. I don't think anyone in her house uses drugs."

"You never know."

"You're right."

"Do you have a way of getting in contact with Tanya?"

"Yes I have her friends number."

"Would you mind calling and asking Tanya to come here so
I could speak with her."

"No problem. Let me get my cell phone out the car."

Ice got up and walked out the house to his car while Mrs. Clark
remained on the sofa and rocked back and forth in disbelief.
He returned to the house with his cell in his hand.

"Mrs. Clark I talked to her I'm gonna run down the block to
pick her up."

"Did you tell her what happened with Anthony?"

"No I just told her you wanted to speak to her."

"Ok let me tell her when she gets here."

"Alright. I'll be right back."

"Thank you Ice."

Ice walked out the house and got in his truck.

"Who the fuck could've gave him that work? This nigga girl pregnant and he's locked up. This nigga Knowledge is gonna bug the fuck out when he here's about this."

These were some of the things that ran through Ice's mind while he drove to Me-Ka's building to pick Tanya up. When Ice arrived at the building Tanya was in front of the building waiting for him. She jumped in the car and asked the question before Ice could drive off.

"Why did he tell his mother?"

"You already knew?"

"Who you think told him I was pregnant?"

"Oh. Nah that's not what she wants to holler at you about."

"What she want then?"

"She wants to be the one to tell you."

"Ice I don't like surprises so can you tell me before we get to his house?"

"Nah she asked me not to tell you."

"Stop playing Ice."

"We almost at his crib chill."

"Aight but you know Me-Ka is sick at you for being late."

"Man this shit is way more important than some date with Me-Ka."

"So this is serious huh?"

"Shit is real right now."

They pulled up in front of Tony's house Tanya spoke up.

"Did something happen to Tony?"

"I told you I was gonna let his moms tell you."

The door was opened so they walked into the house and found Mrs. Clark still sitting on the love seat in deep thought.

"Mrs. Clark." Ice called which caught her attention.

"I'm sorry."

"That's alright."

"Hello Tanya."

"Hi Mrs. Clark."

"Come have a seat. Ice you can sit also."

"Tanya thank you for coming."

"No problem."

"Did Ice tell you what happened?"

"No. He said you wanted to tell me."

"Yes I did. Tonight I received a phone call from a detective at the 120pct. Anthony has been arrested for drugs."

"Drugs?"

"Yes. Ice told me you moved in with your friend."

"Yes today."

"By any chance did Tony come there and take a book bag or a plastic bag?"

"No. When Tony left me earlier he didn't leave with anything."

"Do you know where he went after he left you?"

"He said he was going to drop Ice's truck off and then he was going home."

"Yeah that's the same thing Ice said. Do you know of anyone else's house he could have went to?"

"No. Either he's with Ice or he's with me."

"Alright well he's supposed to go to court tomorrow. When you guys get out of school if you come here or call I'll be able to tell you what the judge said."

"Mrs. Clark Tony is my boy I can miss a day of school for him. I will be there."

"He's right Mrs. Clark I will be there too."

She stood up to give them both a hug.

"Tony is lucky to have a friend like you and a girlfriend like you."

"Mrs. Clark will you need a ride to court in the morning?"

"No I will be alright Ice thank you."

"I am going to leave you my phone number. Call me if you need anything."

"Ok I will."

"Mrs. Clark I'm going to take Tanya home now. I will see you in the morning."

"Thank you both again for coming by."

Ice and Tanya both got in his truck in silence. Tears began to trickle down Tanya's face as she looked at Ice in disgust.

"Why did you give him those drugs?"
Raising his voice.

"What? Yo that's my word Tony didn't get that work from me."

"You was in Tony's house trying to sound all innocent. You got something to do with him being locked up."

"Hold the fuck up you think I got my man locked up? I already told you I had nothing to do with it. I don't appreciate the fact that you in my car accusing me of some bullshit."

"So stop the car I don't need your fucking ride."

Ice pulled over. Tanya got out the car and slammed the passenger's door. Ice pulled off heated because she accused him and he couldn't put her in her place because she's his man's girl.

Ice drove around New Brighton sick trying to relieve himself of the anger he had. He decided to drive to West Brighton to tell Knowledge what went down with Tony. He drove straight up Castelton Avenue and spotted Knowledge in front of Dominos pizzeria disciplining one of his workers. Ice parked his truck and watched Knowledge patiently teach one of his workers a lesson. When Knowledge was finished and walked towards the projects Ice beeped his horn to grab his attention.

"What nigga?"

"I gotta holler at you about Tony."

"Get out the car and show me some respect."

Ice got out his truck nervously not knowing Knowledge's motive.
"Now what happened?"

"I just talked to his moms she said he got locked up."

"For what?"

"The boys bagged him with a bomb."

"Get the fuck out of here. I know he wasn't hustling for you."

"Nah I told you I wasn't giving him a bomb."

"Yeah aight. Yo I gotta go check his moms. It's type late though."

"I just left her crib she was wide awake."

"Fuck it I'm gonna go over there now. You going to court for him tomorrow?"

"Yeah I told his moms I'll meet her there."

"Aight then I'm gone. Yo my fault for screaming on you. That nigga thought he could play with my money."

"It ain't nothing."

They gave each other five and both went there separate ways.

CHAPTER 22

      "All rise as the court receives the honorable judge Mc Kenner."

      "You may be seated. You can call the first case."

      "Case 00784 Anthony Clark vs. the State of New York." Tony walked out stressed in handcuffs and stood next to his attorney.

      "How do you plea?"

      "Guilty."

      "Your honor the defendant is 16 years old I'm asking that the court charges him as an Youthful Offender."

      "Are there any family members present for the defendant?"

      "Yes your honor. The defendant's mother and older brother is here," pointing to Mrs. Clark and Knowledge.

      "Youthful Offender status will be granted. Sentencing will be April 20th at 9am."

      "Call the next case."

Tony was led away by the court officer as he looked at his mother and seen tears seeping from her eyes. Tony's attorney walked out of the courtroom so he could speak with Mrs. Clark and Knowledge. Ice also walked out the courtroom behind them.

      "Mrs. Clark the court will grant Anthony Youthful Offender status which is good."

      "Can you elaborate a little on Youthful Offender status?"

      "Yes. Youthful Offender is a second chance program for kids who have never been in trouble before. After Anthony serves his time his record will be expunged."

      "OK so what is going to happen on his sentencing date?"

      "Well he will be charged with possession of half of an ounce of crack cocaine with the intent to sell. Being that I got the court to grant him Youthful Offender status he will be facing 18 months. At the time of sentencing he will have already served 3 months. I can most likely be able to get his sentencing down to a year."

"OK where will he be held until sentencing?"

"I'm 95% sure Riker's Island but I will give you a call later today when I am 100% sure."

"Alright thank you again for all your help."

"No problem Mrs. Clark. Do you want me to call you at home or at work?"

"I took a week off from work so you can reach me at home."

"Don't worry yourself he'll be fine. I'm going in the back now to speak with Anthony."

"Alright thank you again for your help."

"Your welcome."

They shook hands and Tony's Attorney walked away as Knowledge and Ice escorted Mrs. Clark out of the courthouse.

"Ice thank you for coming."

"No problem."

"I thought Tanya was going to come."

"Mrs. Clark I didn't speak to her. Last night when we left your house we had an argument."

"What for?"

"She accused me of giving Tony the drugs he got arrested with."

"You guys shouldn't be arguing there's nothing we can do now but pray for Anthony."

"You're right."

"If you talk to her make sure you let her know I want to speak with her."

"Alright. I'm going to stop by your house later to find out where Tony will be held."

"Make sure you do because he is going to need your support."

"I will."

Ice gave Mrs. Clark a hug and gave Knowledge a five as he walked to his truck.

Me-Ka walked towards Tanya when she spotted her on the ice cream line in the lunchroom.

"What you doing in school I thought you was going to court for Tony?"

"I was on my way but than I was like fuck it just let me go to school."

"You foul."

"He can't do nothing for me locked up. I gotta do me."

"You ain't no good. You know damn well Tony was hustling to get you some money."

"Well I ain't trying to have a man right now I got my own stress."

"Money B got you going crazy."

"It ain't even him. Before Tony got locked up I said I needed to have some fun."

"That's still foul. Anyway I'll talk to you later. I'm going to class."

Me-Ka walked away disgusted with Tanya. After Tanya ordered her ice cream she walked to the payphone and took Money B's number out of her wallet. She dialed his number with a smile on her face.

"I hope you got my bag."

"Hello."

"Who this?"

With a seductive voice

"Who you want it to be?"

"Stop playing. Who is this?"

"You told me to call when I was lonely."

"Who this Tanya?"

"Yeah."

"My fault I didn't know who you was at first."

"Who got your bag?"

"Nah when I seen the number I thought you was this dude."

"Oh, so what's up with you?"

"Same ol' same ol' you know. I'm on this paper chase right now."

"I hear you."

"Yo why you not in school?"

"I am in school. I got lunch right now."

"Oh aight. Let me handle something. What time you get out of school?"

"2:30."

"Check it I gotta go to the mall today you wanna come with me?"

"Yeah I'll go with you."

"Aight so I'll pick you up from school at 2:30.   Meet me where I seen you and Me-Ka that day."

"Alright bye Money B."

"Later."

They both hung up the phone with excitement. Me-Ka because she knew she could get Money B to trick on her. And Money B because his scam worked to get Tony out the picture.

"That bitch ass nigga's girl on my dick already."

Dorothy and her boyfriend both laid in the nude with satisfaction from the experience they encountered the evening before. When the telephone rang Dorothy sighed with aggravation.

"I do not want to answer that phone."

"Answer it. It may be important."

"It ain't nobody but a bill collector or my job."

"Just answer it."

"Pass me the phone."

Dorothy picked up the phone with animosity.

"Hello."

"You have a collect call from__ Diane. An inmate in a state correctional facility to except these charges press 5 now, otherwise if you do not except hang up."

"I told you it wasn't important."

"Who is it?"

"My sister in jail."

Dorothy angrily dialed 5.

"Hello."

"Hey sis.   I'm sorry for calling so early I wanted to catch you before you went to work."

"I took off today."

"Oh aight.   How's Tanya doing?"

"I haven't seen her in a couple of days."

"Where she at?"

"She moved out."

"With who?"

"I don't know. The girl is pregnant I told her get an abortion or move out. She chose to move out so."

"Dorothy how are you gonna do that to me? You know my baby don't have no where to live."

"Oh well she thinks she's grown so let her get a taste of the real world."

"You don't know where she's staying at?"

"Most likely she's staying at her friend Me-Ka's house but I ain't too sure."

"Do you have Me-Ka's number?"

"Yeah I got it. Hold on."

Dorothy reached on her nightstand for her purse and fondled through it for her address book.

"Hello."

"Yeah."

"You got a pen?"

"Yeah go ahead."

"718-727-7527. I got her address too you want it?"

"Yeah give me that too."

"61 Jersey Street, Apt 4D and she got the same zip code as me."

"What's the girl's whole name?"

"Tameka Williams"

"Nothing for nothing I really think that's fucked up what you did to my daughter."

"Hold up. I took care of her the whole time you was locked up and never once did you send me a dime for her."

"I'm incarcerated how the fuck am I gonna send you money? "Did you forgot whose house you was running to when your so called boyfriend was beating the shit out of you?"

Dorothy hung up the phone with embarrassment because she knew she was wrong for kicking Tanya out. She sat up knowing she was gonna have to answer to her boyfriend.

"Why you kick that little girl out?"

"The little bitch think she's grown."

"You know she ain't got no where to go. Her mother is locked up and her father is dead."

"Oh well."

"You do stupid shit sometimes."

"This is my house I'll do whatever I want."

"Who you raising your voice at?"

"Whatever."

"I told you about speaking to me like I'm a little kid."

"Ain't nobody speaking to you like a little kid."

"Keep playing with me I'm gonna smack the shit out of you."

"I think it's time for you to leave."

"I'll leave whenever I'm ready to fucking leave."

Her boyfriend got out the bed and walked out the room and slammed the door behind him.

"You talk about me doing stupid shit."

Her boyfriend busted back in the room and ran towards her with rage. He snatched her up off the bed by her shoulders and shook her. Talking to her with anger.

"I told you stop talking to me like a little kid."

"Get off of me."

He tossed her on the bed grabbed his clothes and walked towards the door. Before he could get all the way out the door Dorothy launched her pocket book at him, which hit him in the back of his head. He dropped his clothes, turned and charged at her with a vengeance. She tried to run but when he caught her he threw her against the wall and killed all the taste buds in her mouth with his hand. Dorothy swung back but her blow did not phase him. He yoked her up and flung her, which sent her face to face with the dresser. Dorothy lay on the floor crying with agony. He stepped over her; snatched his clothes off the floor, got dressed and walked out the house.

CHAPTER 23

Tanya sat in her last period class anxious for the bell to ring so she could begin her escapade with Money B. When the bell finally did ring she disregarded her daily routine of meeting Me-Ka in front of the water fountain on the second floor. She knew if she told Me-Ka where she was going Me-Ka would definitely try to talk her out of it. Tanya went out the front entrance of the school and walked straight to Money B's car trying to avoid anyone seeing her creeping with him.

"What's up?"

"Nothing I'm chilling."

"You didn't think I was gonna be out here at 2:30 did you?"

"To tell you the truth nah I thought you was gonna have me waiting."

As he pulled off.

"Yo I gotta stop at my house real quick you don't mind do you?"

"Nah go ahead."

"Yo I heard what happened to your man."

"Whoa that's not my man."

"That's not what you told me the other day."

"We had broke up right after I seen you. Then he got locked up that night."

"Damn son had a rough day."

"That's his problem."

"Why yall break up?"

"I told him I needed to have some fun."

"Listen to you. What kind of fun you trying to have?"

"I don't know. I think I just need somebody new to hang out with."

"You gonna let me be that new person?"

"I'm with you right now right?"

"I feel you."

"I just hope you're not boring."

"Nah I like to have fun."

"We'll see."

"You gotta be anywhere today?"

"No why?"

"I want you to hang out with me the rest of the day."

"We can do that if you know how to treat a young lady."

"You're a funny girl."

They rode the rest of the way in silence. When they reached Money B's building he parked the car and they walked into his building.

They rode the elevator while Money B prayed his baby's mother wouldn't be at his door waiting to start an altercation with him. He sighed in relief when he looked ahead and seen an empty doorstep. Money B opened the door for Tanya when she entered she was impressed with his apartment. He told her she could have a seat while he changed his clothes. Tanya sat on the soft brown leather couch and glanced around the apartment in amazement. She reached for the remote and cut on the 42" flat screen TV and thought to herself "I can get used to this."
Money B poked his head out of the bedroom.

"You can get something to drink if you want."
Tanya smiled "Thank you."
She walked into the kitchen so she could survey more of the apartment. She was surprised to see a child's painting on the refrigerator that read I love my daddy. She grabbed a Capri Sun juice out the refrigerator and went back to watching BET in the living room. Money B walked out the bedroom with a Roc-A-Wear jean suit and a crisp pair of construction Timberlands.

"You ready?"

"Yeah."
Tanya turned off the TV and followed Money B to the door.
They walked back to the car and Money B wondered how she felt about his sons drawing on the refrigerator.

"You have a nice house Money B."
As he drove off towards the mall

"Thanks. I'm about to redo it though."

"Why?"

"I get tired of stuff quick."

"I hear that."

"Nah not like that. I just like to feel comfortable in my house."

"Oh."

"There you go. You was ready to say drive me home."

"You damn right. I didn't like the way that sounded."

"Nah you good I was feeling you since I seen you that night in the Wave."

"Yeah aight. You damn sure didn't act like it that night. I only seen you when you walked in and Me-Ka introduced us."

"Nah I got the report you was in there with your man so I had to fall back."

"Please."

"What you mean? I had to respect that."

"You wasn't feeling me that hard. What if that was you're last time seeing me?"

"I did my homework."

"What homework you did?"

"The streets gave me your resume."

"Yeah right. So what you know?"

"I know you're the only child, you a junior in high school, you lived in the red houses but you just moved."

"How you know I just moved?"

"I'm telling you I did my homework."

"Me-Ka had to tell you that."

"I haven't seen Me-Ka."

"So who told you?"

"I can't reveal my sources."

On the ride to the mall they talked and got comfortable with each other. Tanya was happy because her plan of getting him to trick on her was becoming easier. Money B was excited because although she was young he found potential in Tanya to wife her.

Me-Ka sat in her bedroom looking at college application stressed because it was her senior year and she had not applied to a college yet. She was interrupted by her main distraction the ringing of the telephone.

"Hello."

"You have a collect call from Diane. An inmate in a state correctional facility to except these charges press 5 now, otherwise if you do not except hang up now."

"This must be Tanya's mother."

Me-Ka dialed five.

"Hello."

"Hi this is Diane Tanya's mother may I speak to Tameka please?"

"This is her."

"I'm sorry for calling but I got your number from my sister. She told me that Tanya maybe staying with you."

"Yes. She moved in the day before yesterday."

"I just want to thank you so much for letting her stay there with you."

"Its no problem Tanya is my home girl."

"Please let your mother know I appreciate it so much."

"I will."

"Is Tanya there now?"

"No I don't know where she went I was waiting for her after school but I didn't see her."

"She's probably with her boyfriend."

"I know for a fact she's not with him. He got locked up the other day."

"For what?"

"Drugs."

"Damn. But listen I don't want to run your mothers phone bill up but please do me a favor let Tanya know I love her so much and that I'm sending her a letter to your house."

"Do you have the address?"

"Yes my sister gave it to me?"

"Alright I'll let her know."

"Make sure you tell your mother I said thank you."

"I will."

"Bye."

Me-Ka hung up the phone and went back to reading the criteria for colleges she wanted to attend. She was again interrupted by a knock at her front door. Me-Ka looked through the peephole and was thrilled to see Ice on the other side of the door. She quickly unlocked the door and invited him in.

"What a surprise."

"You still mad?"

"Nah. I heard what happened with your man."

"Yeah that shit got me going crazy."

"Come in my room we can talk in there."

"Your peoples here?"

"No. What brings you down here?"

"I came to put your friend in her place."

"Why what happened?"

"She probably told you already but she tried to blame Tony's arrest on me."

"Nah she didn't tell me that."

"Yeah she losing her mind. After that she didn't even come to court today for him."

"I know. I saw her in school today and I told her she was foul."

"She on some bullshit. If he was hustling it was for her."

"I told her that. Tony ain't never try to hustle before until her aunt kicked her out."

"I hope she don't try to dis my man since he's locked up."

"Between you and me I think she's creeping right now."

"With who?"

"You gotta give me your word you won't say nothing."

"That's my word."

"I think she's feeling the kid Money B."

"Say word."

"Yeah he been hollering at her."

"Get the fuck out of here."

"I'm telling you."

"I ain't tryin to let that go down."

"There ain't nothing you can do."

"Nah my man locked up I can't let his chick do him dirty like that."

"Remember you said you wasn't gonna say nothing."

"I ain't. Fuck it what you doing right now?"

"Nothing really I was looking at these college applications."

"That's right my baby girl about to leave me."

"Please you got too many chicks for me to be your baby girl."

Ice walked towards Me-Ka wrapped his arms around her and started kissing her neck.

"Don't start nothing you can't finish."

"You know I can finish it."

Me-Ka pushed him off her.

"I told you, you had a lot of making up to do."

"You a funny girl."

"What you thought I was one of your little groupies?"

"There you go. Are you doin anything right now?"

"I told you what I was doin."

"Come take a ride with me."

"Where too?"

"I wanna pick some jeans and sneakers up from the mall."

"What's in it for me?"

"You get to be in my presence."

"Please, I'll pass."

"You know you can get something."

"Nah I don't want nothing just get me something to eat."

"No question. I'm starving my damn self."

"Let me throw some sweats on then we can be out."

"What's wrong with them jeans?"

"Nothing I just wanna get comfortable."

Me-Ka reached in her dresser and pulled out a pair of gray sweat pants. She unbuckled her belt and jeans and pulled them down in front of Ice revealing her leopard thong. Ice's man was stimulated with the sight of her thong.

"You trying to tease me?"

"No. You seen it already so I don't have to hide it."

"The last time I seen it I was in it."

"You could be in it right now if you knew how to act."

Me-Ka pulled her sweat pants over her buttocks and smiled as she noticed the swelling in Ice's jeans. She put on her sneakers and grabbed a jacket out of her closet.

"You ready?"

"Yeah come on."

They drove to the mall laughing and listening to the best of R-Kelly. When they got to the mall they shopped around for a little while. Ice copped a pair of white uptowns and a pair of field boot Timberlands. Their hunger caused them to stop shopping and get something to eat. They both decided on Wendy's so they took the escalator upstairs. When they got off the escalator Me-Ka spotted Tanya and Money B in the Steve Madden store looking at shoes.

"Yo walk back pass Steve Madden and look in."

"For what?"

"Just go ahead."

Ice did it and the expression on his face showed that he was pissed off. He started to walk into the store but Me-Ka grabbed him.

"Fuck it just let them be."

"Nah that bitch is trying to play my man."

"Now we know how she is."

"Yo let me get the fuck out the mall before I kill this nigga."

"Come on there's a Wendy's on the way home."

They got back in the truck Ice sped down Richmond Avenue and hopped on the Staten Island Expressway. He maneuvered his way through traffic and they got back to New Brighton in fifteen minutes.

"You want me to drop you off or you gonna chill with me?"

"Nah I'll chill for a little while."

"Yo let me stop at Tony's mom's crib then we can order something to eat from my crib."

"I know you ain't gonna tell her about Tanya."

"Fuck that bitch. I told her I was gonna stop by to get his address."

"Oh."

Ice pulled up in front of Mrs. Clark's house and got out leaving the truck running.

"I'll be right back."

"Don't have me out here all day."

"Shut up."

Ice walked onto the porch and rung the bell. Mrs. Clark took her time answering the door so Ice rung the bell again. She opened the door with a joyful face.

"I knew that was you. I heard your music a block away." Smiling.

"How you doing Mrs. Clark?"

"Well I had better days   but all I can do now is pray."

"Mrs. Clark don't worry yourself Tony will be alright."

"I hope so."

"Did the lawyer call you with Tony's address?"

"Yes I wrote it out for you. Anthony called a little while ago."

"Yeah. How's he holding up?"

"He said he was ok but he sounds stressed."

"Hopefully that will ware off."

"He's on Riker's Island he said he's in a house with a couple of people he knows from Staten Island."

"Oh that's good then."

"Wait one minute let me get you the address off the table."

Mrs. Clark walked off and Ice noticed a couple of photo albums on the sofa.

"She must've been in here reminiscing."

Mrs. Clark returned with the address and her smile.

"I see you were looking at some pictures."

"Yeah. It's not easy."

"I understand."

"I have a boy in the grave and a boy in jail. I have nothing left."

"Mrs. Clark Tony will be home in no time."

"I know. Here's his address he said he's waiting to hear from you."

"Alright Mrs. Clark I have my friend in the car waiting."

"Ice stay out of trouble."

"I will. I'm gonna stop by during the week to see you."

"Please do."

Mrs. Clark walked Ice to the door and gave him a hug as he walked out of her home. When he got back in the truck Me-Ka was shaking her head.

"I don't know why you shaking your head."

"Because I told you not to have me out here waiting forever."

"Shut up I was in there for five minutes."

"You and his moms are cool?"

"Yeah me and Tony been cool for a minute. His moms and my moms use to go to the same church."

"Oh I thought yall just met each other."

"That was always my man. You know I'm older than him so I was in the streets two years before him."

"That's probably why I thought yall just met each other."

Ice pulled up in front of his house they both got out and went inside. Me-Ka made herself comfortable while Ice put his footwear away."

"You be getting real comfortable in my house."

"Please I run this."

"You don't run nothing but them laps in your gym class."

Smiling.

"You got jokes?"

"No jokes. What you want to eat?"

"I think I want some Chinese food."

"There is a menu on the table go order it."

Walking to get the menu.

"What you want?"

"Get me some General Tso chicken and fried rice."

Dialing the phone number.

"I'm about to order the whole left side."

"And you gonna be paying for the whole left side."

Me-Ka ordered the food and returned to the sofa to join Ice.

"What you watching?"

"I don't know what this is but why the fuck you acting like a stranger?"

"How you figure?"

"You sitting all the way over there like I stink or something"

Getting up to sit next to him. "Shut up."

Ice placed his arm around her shoulder and went back to watching the movie. After a while Ice's hormones encouraged him to try to seduce her. Ice leaned over and began kissing her on her neck. Surprisingly she didn't refuse his touch. She sat on the couch and enjoyed every lick and kiss. Ice took it a step further he reached under her T-shirt and caressed her breast. With her first moan of affection Ice laid her on the sofa and began circulating his tongue about her stomach. He lifted her bra and aggressively sucked her breast. Ice ran his tongue down her belly to the tip of her sweat pants. With the help of his hands he used his tongue to pull down her sweats. He elevated her legs in the air and removed her pants and footwear. Me-Ka laid on the sofa with her firm dark chocolate thighs exposed. Ice turned Me-Ka over on her stomach staring at the thong that caught his attention earlier. He licked up her inner thighs in a circular motion until he felt the heat from her womb. Ice released her vagina from her thong and made her vagina moist by teasing her with his index finger. When Me-Ka's womb was dripping with desire, spreading her legs Ice had a drink from her fountain of love. He maneuvered his tongue in a wave like motion around her clitoris, which caused Me-Ka to loose an exotic groan. Ice closed his eyes and proved to her that he had skills. He was able to operate his tongue at different paces. He had no intention of ending his technique until he heard their Chinese food being delivered. The amount of love Ice drank from her fountain made Me-Ka feel as if she was in heaven. Me-Ka didn't know but Ice's nickname was Hurricane Tongue.

Chapter 24
7 Months Later

    October 21 she refused to take any medication so she lay in St. Vincent's Hospital screaming from the excruciating pain that she endured by giving birth to her child. The child's stepfather stood in the room having his hand squeezed experiencing this wonderful moment in her life. After eight hours of strenuous labor she brought a healthy baby into the world. This happy couple agreed to name their baby girl Destiny. The next morning although Me-ka was not fond of the couple she came to visit the newborn baby. Money B sat on the side of the bed talking with Tanya when Me-Ka entered the room he got up and walked out of the room.

    "Hey Me-Ka what's up?"

    "I'm chilling. How you doing?"

    "I'm alright. Just tired."

    "You still in pain?"

    "Not really. Every now and then I'll feel some pain."

    "I stopped by the nursery when I came. She is so beautiful."

    "Yeah that's my little lady."

    "Where did you get the name Destiny?"

    "You know where I got it from."

Smiling.

    "Yeah that was me."

    "I haven't talked to you in a minute."

    "That's because you don't love me no more."

    "Stop it. It's just I live in Stapelton now and you live in New Brighton."

    "How is it in Stapelton?"

    "Its aight. I'm rarely outside. I just walk through."

    "Are them chicks still hating out there?"

    "Now its just his baby's mother. She be calling the house acting stupid."

"You know that ain't nothing. Oh boy about to come home."

"Yeah I know how much longer he got?"

"I talked to him yesterday he said he'll be home in two and a half months."

"I just hope him and Money B don't get in to it."

"All he's talking about is seeing his child. He said if yall happy then he happy."

"I seen his mother on the ferry one day it looked like she wanted to spit in my face."

"You know that's her baby boy."

"I know. How's college going?"

"It's alright. I do a whole lot of reading."

"Somebody had asked me if you went to the St. John's on Staten Island or the one in Queens. I couldn't tell them."

"Nah I go to the one out here. I'm thinking about transferring to the one in Queens next year."

"You don't like this one out here?"

"It's not that. I'm like the only black person on the campus."

"Oh yeah you gotta transfer."

Standing up.

"But let me go so you can get some rest. Call me when you get out the hospital so I can come see the baby."

"Alright. If you speak to Tony let him know what I named her and tell him I'm gonna give you some pictures so you can send them to him."

"I will. I'm supposed to go see him but I be crazy busy with school."

Tanya leaned over the bed and gave Me-Ka a hug and kiss.

"Make sure you call me so I can come see the baby."

"I will."

"Alright take care."

Walking out of the room Me-Ka bumped into Money B and shook her head as they made eye contact. Me-Ka didn't want to come to the hospital but out of respect for the baby she stopped by. Her conversation was very brief with Tanya because she was pissed off with her for playing Tony. She had to get out of that room because she felt she was being phony.

Knowledge and Ice sat in Ice's truck in front of the check cashing conversing. They had bumped into each other buying Money Orders to send to Tony. Over the past few months they became cool. Knowledge like the way Ice stepped up for his, their man Tony. Every week Ice made sure he sent Tony a package and made sure his commissary was sexy.

"Yeah I heard that chick Tony was fucking with went into labor."

"I heard that shit too. Fuck that bitch."

"You know Tony is gonna have problems with the nigga Money B when he come home?"

"I know he's already talking about when he come home he's gonna want to see his baby."

"The nigga Money B ain't gonna want Tony calling and coming to his crib."

"Man listen it's gonna get ugly."

"Tell you the truth I think Money B set Tony up."

"I was thinking the same thing. Tony still won't tell me who he was hustling for."

"Every time I ask him he changes the subject."

"Yo he's still getting paroled to your crib?"

"Yeah he said he ain't trying to move to Connecticut with his moms."

"I don't blame him."

"But yo my man is having a party at Secrets tomorrow come through."

"Nah I don't feel right in them clubs without my man."

"I feel you."

"Next time I'll be in a club is when my dog comes home."

"I hear you. Let me slide today is collection day. These niggas gotta pay their taxes."

"Get that Money!"

"What you doing today?"

"Nothing I'm about to go get a shape up."

"From where?"

"The best barber on Staten Island."

"Who Sean?"

"You know it."

"Yall New Brighton niggas are crazy my man in West Brighton is nice."

"I don't care what you say he can't fuck with Sean."

"Whatever nigga I'm gone."

Giving each other a five.   "1000."

Ice drove to the barbershop thinking about his conversation with Knowledge about Money B setting Tony up.

"If that's the case Tony is gonna have to get papers on the nigga head."

Ice parked his truck at the meters in front of the shop and walked in the shop surprised to see Sean wasn't cutting anybody.

"What business is slow today?"

"These niggas didn't get their checks yet."

"Shit I need to come in here around this time more often."

"The first and the fifteenth is when business is really crazy."

"Yeah that's when them disability checks come in."

"What you getting a shape up?"

"Yeah."

"What's up with Tony?"

"He good. He's on a count down now."

"How much longer he got?"

"He'll be home the beginning of January."

"That's cool. That chick had the baby yet?"

"She went into the hospital the other day but I don't know if she had it yet."

"Shorty is no good."

"Fuck that chick."

"I know Tony is sick."

"You know he was in love so that shit fucked him up."

"What's crazy is she played him at his weakest point."

"The way I see it she was messing with the nigga Money B for a minute because the day after he got locked up I seen her in the mall with the nigga."

"Say word."

"That's my word. She wasted no time."

"That's a damn shame."

"Word she was waiting for the right moment. When the nigga got locked up that was it."

"Everything that glitters ain't gold."

"You ain't never lie."

"Fuck it though. I'll probably throw a party for him when he come home."

"That's cool. If you need flyers you know Tariq got the

shop."

"That's right I forgot the God got that shop. What's the name of it again?"

"Uniquest. Its over there on Van Duzer Street."

"Yeah I'm a definitely let him do the flyers if I have the party." Handing Ice a mirror.

"What's up with you though?"

"Real quiet right now. Yo I just had an argument with my man Knowledge about you."

"About what?"

"He tried to tell me there's some kid in West Brighton better than you."

"Yeah aight you know who Staten Island's finest is." Handing Sean a twenty-dollar bill.

"That's what I was trying to tell the dude."

"Good looking. You need to bring him through and let me cut him he'll understand."

"I know but let me get out of here."

Ice drove home trying to calculate his next re-up. His math was interrupted when he reached his house and seen his mother in front of their house talking to the blue and whites. He parked the truck got out not knowing what to expect.

"Ma what happened?"

"Somebody tried to break in the house through the basement."

"When just now?"

"A little while ago."

"Did they get in?"

"No they broke the side window and the lady next door started screaming and they ran."

"She seen who it was?"

"She said it was two young kids. Let me finish talking to these cops and I'll come in the house and talk to you."

Ice went in the house heated. The first thing he did was counted the money in the stash. He was relieved a little when his count came up correct. Ice heard his mother walking down the steps so he put the money back in the stash. She walked in the basement and joined him on the couch.

"Ma you aight?"

"I'm fine. Luckily the lady next door was home because I

didn't hear the window break."

"Yeah."

"You know you gotta lay low for a little while."

"For what?"

"You got people trying to rob you."

"Ma I'm good I ain't worrying about these little dudes."

"Don't make no more sells out the house. You're making the house hot."

"Ma I don't have drugs in here I just keep money here."

"You have to move it. Keep a little here and move the safe some where else."

"Aight."

"Did you go in the safe when somebody was here?"

"Nah I don't think so."

"Ice you are getting sloppy. Watch who you bring in the house."

"Don't nobody be in here."

"I'm talking about them little girls too. They'll set you up in a minute."

"I know."

Walking towards the steps.

"You say you know. How's Tony doing?"

"He's good I'm supposed to go see him."

"That's a damn shame you didn't go see that boy yet."

"Whatever. I make sure he's eating though."

"Yeah Yeah. Ice be careful out there."

"I will."

Ice sat on the sofa and picked his brain about who could've tried to rob him. The only stick-up kids on Staten Island were Money B's soldiers.

"He's gonna make me get on some real Murder 1 shit."

Chapter 25

January 3rd Ice stood on 42nd Street in the city at the Port Authority waiting for Tony to get off the state bus. It seemed like he had been there all day but he waited anxiously for his man to touch down. Ice no longer complained once Tony walked off the bus and they made eye contact. He almost didn't recognize him. He wasn't use to seeing Tony without waves. They both had smiles on their face as they approached each other. Giving each other a hug.

"What's really good?"

"What's good really?"

"I'm just happy to be home."

"I feel you kid. Welcome home."

"Yo why you never came to see me?"

As they started walking towards Ice's truck.

"God I wasn't trying to see you in a cage."

"I respect that."

"What you want to do tonight?"

"Nah I gotta lay low tonight. My moms came from Connecticut to see me."

"Oh word that's cool."

"Word. She got me a room at the Staten Island Hotel. We supposed to go to dinner and shit."

"God what's good with your hair?"

"I know. I wasn't trying to let them dweeb ass niggas cut my shit."

"I gotta get you to Sean quick."

"Word. My moms will flip if she see my hair like this."

"Son you ain't gonna recognize my whip."

"What you do to it?"

"I just threw some feet on it."

"Ice I know that ain't your shit right there."

"Yeah that's it."

"That's them Sprewell shits right?"

"Yeah."

"What size rims are these?"

"Deuce four."

"Niggas told me you was getting money but I didn't know it was like that."

They gave each other five as they got in the truck and headed towards Staten Island.

"You know I gotta hurt the streets."

"I feel you."

"If I don't do it who's gonna do it?"

"Do it playboy. Yo I got some paper for you too."

"What you talking about?"

"The extra money that was in my commissary."

"Nah keep that kid. That's you."

"Good looking."

"Yo Knowledge is supposed to take you shopping whatever else you need I got you."

"Good looking my nigga. Soon as I get on my feet I'm gonna hit you right back."

"Don't sweat that. I'm on my feet so you on your feet"

"Yo you seen my daughter yet?"

"Nah. Tell you the truth I tried to keep my distance from your baby moms."

"I feel you. I'm trying to keep my distance too. I just want to see my daughter."

"Yeah."

"You know I'm gonna have to see that faggot ass nigga Money B."

"Fuck him. As soon as she sees you doing it she's gonna jump right back on your dick."

"I ain't tripping about her. You know the nigga a snitch."

"Nigga I was asking you that. I would've been handle the nigga."

"Nah I knew I could've pushed buttons while I was locked up but I wanted to see it done while I was in the streets."

"I'm gonna get one of them little young niggas on it right away."

"Nah I want him to think everything is sweet, then I'm gonna pop his fuckin head off his shoulders. God he had me heated when I was locked up. The nigga snitched on me because he wanted my chick that's a bitch move."

"Yo I told you not to fuck with him. I told you he was grimy."

"Yeah I know. Remember when Tanya got kicked out her crib. I was trying to be a good nigga and get some paper so we could get a little apartment. I stepped to Knowledge for some work he deaded me. I knew you wasn't gonna give me a bomb, so I got at that nigga. He gave me a bomb and called the boys as soon as he gave it to me."

"That's a damn shame dudes be snitching like that."

"Man there are so many snitches out there you don't know who to trust."

"Knowledge told me your record was suppose to get erased but you was fighting or something so it's sticking with you."

"Yeah remember that day in court my attorney asked for Youthful Offender status?"

"Yeah."

"With that shit my record was supposed to be erased but I had   a couple of fights with these German niggas the court took that shit right from me."

"Damn God you fucked up."

"Nah I'll be aight. I kicked it with Knowledge I got a little plan for the streets. I'm gonna build with you later on."

"No question."

They drove over the Verrazano Bridge in silence when they reached the tollbooth.

"Yo you got Sean's number?"

"Yeah."

"Dial his number for me."

Ice dialed the barbershop number than handed Tony his cell phone.

"Barbershop."

"Can I speak to Sean?"

"This is him."

"Peace God. Yo I been locked up for a year without a hair cut I know I can slide in your chair."

"Who this Tony?"

"You know this is Tony."

"Welcome home kid. Yeah come through."

"Yo I gotta handle something so I gotta get right in the chair."

"Aight. How long is it gonna take you to get here?"
"I just got off the bridge. I can be there in five minutes."
"Yeah come through your next."
"That's what I'm talking about good looking."
"1."

Tony hung up the phone with a smile.
"What he said?"
"He said I'm next."
"That's whats up because your shit is foul."
"Give me two days and the waves will be spinning again."
"Hell no them shits are through."
"Watch and learn the kid got good hair."
"We'll see."
"Yo what up with you and Me-Ka?"
"Nothing kid. I haven't seen her in a minute."
"Their yall go with that bullshit again."
"Nah we ain't beefing. She doing her thing with school and you know I been grinding hard."
"I feel you. Yall will be back together in a minute."
"Nah I think that's it kid. I been there done that plus I got the hottest thing walking the streets."
"Who?"
"Shorty moms from the Harbor but she live in Jersey. I'm gonna bring her through so you can meet her."
"She might be aight but she ain't the hottest thing walking."
"I'm telling you kid the hottest thing walking."
"She can't be if she mess with you."
"You sleeping on my pimp game?"
"I been told you, you ain't no pimp you're an assistant pimp."
Both were laughing as they pulled up in front of the barbershop.
"Get out."
"Let me get my shit done up so I can bag your girl."
"Never."
"Yo you gonna come back for me right?"
"Yeah. You acting like you don't know where you at. You only been locked up for a year."
"Stop playing God."
"Nah I'm going to my crib I'll be right back."

"Smooth."

Tony got his hair cut and his wig was looking official. He stood outside the shop waiting for Ice to return. After a good ten-minutes, Ice pulled up to pick him up.

"I thought you was coming right back."

"Get in the car and shut up."

"You never on time."

"Where you want me to drive you to?"

"To the Staten Island Hotel I gotta meet my moms out there."

"When I was walking out my crib to pick you up one of my soldiers called me. I had to bring him a pack."

"Oh aight."

"As long as you didn't have me out here waiting because of some bitch."

"So what's good you're gonna kick it with your moms tonight or you want me to come scoop you later?"

"Nah I'm gonna go to dinner with her then go to sleep, I'm starting the grind early in the morning."

As they got on the Staten Island Expressway.

"I feel you. What plans you got?"

"Oh yeah. Knowledge is gonna front me a brick. He set me up with a spot in New Brighton in 456 and I'm gonna kill the streets with the two for five."

"It sounds good."

"My nigga it is good."

"What you gonna do about the hustlers whose toes you stepping on?"

"Knowledge took care of that already them clowns out there know. Like Beans said either they gonna get down or lay down."

"I feel you."

"It's my turn. We about to be the trilogy. You got the weed sells on smash. I'm gonna have the crack game sewed up and you know Knowledge is hurting West Brighton."

"Just make sure you don't get sloppy."

"Believe me I know. Everybody else has been eating. It's my time around."

"You know you got my support."

"No question. I appreciate that."

"But for real what do you want to do about Money B?"

"Keep it quiet right now. Lets get this money than we will handle him."

"Aight but he gotta get it."

"Believe me when I go get him I'm going head hunting."

"We gotta leave him where he stands because he likes running to the police."

"What you thought I was gonna hit him in the leg, I'm not playing with that dude."

"Aight."

Ice pulled up to the door of the Staten Island Hotel.

"What you gotta do tomorrow?"

"Nothing. Why what up?"

"I might need your help with something."

"With what?"

"Chill out you thirsty. I'll holler at you tomorrow."

"That's peace. Welcome home kid."

"Thanks and I really do appreciate you holding me down while I was locked up."

"That ain't about nothing. We family. I know you would do the same for me if the shoe was on the other foot."

"No question."

"Yo tell your moms I said hi."

Giving Ice a five and getting out of the truck.

"Aight. I'm gonna holler at you tomorrow."

"1000."

Chapter 26

Tony walked into the hotel and made his way to the front desk.

"Hi I'm here to visit my mother Mrs. Clark."

"Yes she's in the first floor lounge waiting your arrival."

"Thank you."

Tony paced his self to the elevator not knowing the type of vibe his mother was going to show him. He knew he had let her down. She had high expectations for him but his love for Tanya deleted all of his mother's hopes and dreams. Tony walked off the elevator with his heart beating at an irregular speed. He entered the lounge and was greeted by his mother's gladdened expression. Mrs. Clark stood up and gave her son a big hug and kiss. She relieved built up stress and hurt with that hug and kiss.

"Hey ma how you doing?"

"I'm ok how are you?"

"I'm good."

"Why did you gain so much weight?"

"I didn't gain that much weight."

"Yes you did when you left I was able to wrap my arms around my baby."

"You can still wrap your arms around me."

"Barely."

"How you like it up in Connecticut?"

"I love it. I brought you some pictures of the house."

"I can't wait to get up there. As soon as my parole officer gives me the word I'm gonna fly up there."

"I hope so. You will love it up there."

"I'm just trying to get a home cook meal."

Laughing.

"I haven't had a reason to cook in so long."

"Well your baby is home. I'm your reason."

"I know and I missed you so much."

"I missed you too. I'm sorry I had you worrying."

"Don't be sorry just learn from your mistakes."

"I will."

"Talking about food you made me hungry. Did you eat yet?"

"No. I was waiting to eat with you."

"Where do you want to go to eat?"

"You can pick the place."

"No. This is your first meal home where do you want to go?"

"Ma we don't have to go any where fancy. Doesn't the hotel have a restaurant?

"Yes. You want to go down stairs?"

"Yeah that's cool with me."

Tony and his mother dined in the hotel restaurant they conversed over dinner. Mrs. Clark made Tony promise that he would stay out of trouble. She also made him confess that he was the father of Tanya's baby. She made it clear to him that, that day was the best day she had in a year's time. Her baby boy was home from prison and she had finally received the news that she was a grandmother. After dinner Tony walked his mother to her car so she could start her journey to Connecticut. When she pulled off Tony checked into his room and quickly took a shower anxious to use the toiletries his mother purchased for him. After his shower Tony laid on the bed naked something he chose not to do while he was incarcerated. Like every other heterosexual male their first night home from a penitentiary Tony wanted to be between a pair of warm female legs.

Before his incarceration his only love was the girl he lost his virginity to. He knew she was out of the question so he sat on the bed hormones running rampant thinking of who he could call to unclog his pipe. He only kept in contact with one female while he was locked up so his only choice was to draft Me-Ka. He dialed her number praying she would answer. When he was about to call it quits she picked up on the fourth ring.

"Hello."

"You was sleep?"

"I just laid down."

"You don't even know who you're speaking to."

"Your right who is this?"

"This is Tony."

With enthusiasm

"Oh hey. You home?"

"You sound real excited. Yeah the kid is home."

"Yeah I'm excited you're home. When did you come home?"

"I touched down earlier today."

"You told me you was gonna call me as soon as you got to the Island."

"I know I was thinking about you. I had to do some running around. You know how that goes."

"I feel you. Where you at now?"

"I just got finished eating with my moms. She got me a room at the Staten Island Hotel."

"Oh word that's peace. All your peoples up there?"

"Nah I'm by myself. I needed a day to relax my mind."

"I feel you."

"So what's up. What you doing right now?"

"I told you I just laid down."

"I'm trying to see you. Come share this luxury with me."

"Nah Tony I got school in the morning. I gotta get up early."

"I ain't trying to hear that. Your boy is home you can be tired tomorrow for me."

"I mean I want to see you but how would your boy feel about that?"

"Listen he can't be mad if two friends chill with each other."

"I don't know."

"Me-Ka don't do me dirty."

"I ain't trying to do you dirty I just don't want your boy to find out or your baby mother."

"Nah this is between me and you. You know nobody is gonna see you all the way out here."

"You right. Tony that's my word you better not say nothing to your boy."

"My word is bond."

"Aight. I'll be there in like a half. What room you in?"

"410, go to the front desk when you get here they will call my room."

"Aight let me throw something on I'll be there."

"Don't have me waiting for you and you don't come."

"Nah that's my word I'm on my way."

"Aight 1."

Tony hung up the phone with a smile ear to ear. The time he waited seemed like the longest half an hour in the world. He sat on the bed watching ESPN with one hand on the phone waiting for it to ring.

When the phone finally rang he picked it up before the first ring was complete. He confirmed Me-Ka as a visitor to the desk attendant and put on a pair of basketball shorts as he propped open the door for Me-Ka. Tony didn't want to look thirsty to Me-Ka so he looked in the mirror until she made her way into the room. She spotted him in the bathroom without a shirt on and made a mental note.

"He can definitely get it."

They walked towards each other and greeted one another with a hug and friendly kiss.

"You didn't think I was gonna come huh?"

"Nah I had faith in you."

As they walked out the bathroom

"Yeah right. What you just got out the shower?"

"A little while ago."

"How did you get so big?"

"I was so bored I was doing a1000 push ups and 1000 sit-ups a day."

"Damn."

"What it don't look good?"

"Nah I like it." Catching herself, "It looks good."

Smiling.

"Take your coat off."

"What time do you have to check out in the morning?"

"By 11:00."

"Do you mind if I leave for school from here?"

"Stop asking stupid questions. You know damn well I don't care."

"I don't know you might kick me out in a hour or two for one of your chicks."

"Nah you my nigga you come before any bird."

"I better. You got me out my bed and I'm dead tired."

"So lay down."

"I'm about to. I'm tired as shit."

"Yeah I gotta get up early to."

"What time?"

"I gotta be in the hood at 7:00."

"Damn so that means you gotta get up like 6:00."

"So why you tell me to come through?"

"I told you I wanted to see you. You don't have to leave that early. You can order room service. When you leave just tell the desk that you checking out."

"Aight. I'm about to change my clothes and lay down."

"Go ahead."

Me-Ka got off the bed and walked into the bathroom with the plastic bag she came in with. While she was changing her clothes Tony cut off the lights, laid in the bed and anticipated what she was going to model to bed. Me-Ka took off her leopard thong and put on a pair of Black Victoria Secret lace boy shorts to match the bra she had on. She stared in the mirror happy with her reflection.

"This nigga might bust as soon as he sees me with this shit on."

Me-Ka took her time in the bathroom before she walked out she sprayed herself with Victoria Secret Pear body splash. When she exited the bathroom she walked across the room as if she was modeling in a Lingerie fashion show scene. Tony followed her every move with the light that was beaming in from the streetlights. At the site of her body his manhood was erect and ready to erupt. Me-Ka got in the bed and made herself comfortable against his back. As she planned Tony turned around and they lay face to face. Me-Ka noticed his hesitance and grabbed his arm and wrapped it around her. "Don't be scared you can hold me". Tony happy and embarrassed because he knew she felt his manhood at attention.

"What's that poking me?"

"I don't know what you're talking about."

Me-Ka walking her fingers down his abs and into his shorts grabbing his pipe. Agreeing with Tanya when she said he was packing.

"What's this?"

Eyes rolling in the back of his head.

"You tell me."

Me-Ka knew she wasn't gonna get much out of him because he was inactive for a year hopefully. She lay on his chest.

"The last time we was like this you was on top but you didn't make a move."

Tony lay there like he was a virgin with an experienced girl. Me-Ka took control of the situation. She kissed and sucked on his neck until he jumped thinking she was gonna give him a hickey. She smiled and ran her tongue down his chest halting to suck on his nipples. Tony lay there enjoying the saliva and warmth of her body. Me-Ka slowly and passionately licked his stomach sucking each ripple looking up into his eyes. She stood up on the bed stepped out of her boy shorts and unloosened her bra. Tony stared at her breast and was amazed how perfect they laid as she threw her bra on the floor. Me-Ka gazing into his eyes knowing she had his undivided attention began to dance for him. She bit her bottom lip as she moved her body slowly to an unheard beat. While dancing she sensually massaged her breast never loosing eye contact with him. With her nipples harden she leaned over and sucked her fully matured breast leaving Tony yearning her touch. Continuing to dance Me-Ka enticingly shifted her hands down her physique ending her dancing as she bent down kneeling over Tony's body. With his penis erect she placed it between her breast and began to jerk it hoping he wouldn't explode yet. With feeling his pre-discharge on her chest she did what she knew he desired. Me-Ka grabbed his cock and placed it in her mouth sucking it softly but with speed. Before she could complete her fifth stroke his toes curled and Me-Ka had recess in her mouth. Tony crawled into the fetal position and trembled with excitement. Me-Ka still had a burning desire to feel his penis fill up her vagina so she walked to the chair looked through her plastic bag and retrieved a 12-inch vibrating dildo. Me-Ka walked back to the bed leaned next to his trembling body and performed what she wanted to feel from Tony with the dildo. Tony looked in amazement as Me-Ka stood next to him in the doggy style position ramming the dildo into her saturated vagina. Tony listened to her, as her heavy breathing became moans, which caused his penis to bulge up again. He stood up and walked behind her removed the dildo from her hand and went skinny-dipping into her vagina. Tony's penis did exactly what she desired. It expanded her vagina to the max, as he sent thrust to her uterus. Me-Ka threw it back like a pro as Tony tried to keep up with her rhythm. She dug her nails into the sheets and released a roar as he slapped her on the ass and tried to push his cock into her deeper. Me-Ka felt an orgasm coming on as Tony began to slow his rhythm up. She begged him not to stop and demand that he stroked faster. He stroked faster and at the last minute he tried to pull out of her but it was too late. Me-Ka grabbed his penis out of her and placed the vibrating dildo on her clitoris, so she could feel what Tony was experiencing. After a few moments she laid on the bed feeling like she was soaring. Tony went to the bathroom washed up and joined her on the bed. Both appeased with one another's performance they snuggled with each other and went to sleep. The next morning Tony jumped up out the bed at 9:30 mad that he was late for his appointment. He got dressed and woke Me-Ka up not knowing what time she had to be at school.

"Yo what time you got class?"

"8:15."

"Shit you missed that class."

"What time is it?"

"9:40."

Getting out of the bed.

"Get the fuck out of here. I thought you had to be somewhere at 7:00?"

"I did. I just woke up my damn self."

"I knew I shouldn't have fucked with you."

"Why?"

"You made me miss my first class."

"How I make you late?"

"You threw it on me and I couldn't get up for my class."

"So that means it's your fault why I'm late."

"How you figure?"

"You turned me out and now I'm late."

"Whatever. You still going where you had to go?"

"I don't know let me call my man."

Tony dialed Knowledge number as Me-Ka walked into the bathroom.

"Hello."

"What up God?"

"Where you at?"

"I just woke up I'm still in the hotel."

"You used to them hard ass beds up north. You couldn't get out that hotel bed huh?"

"Word I was dead to the world."

"Yo I'm down here now watching these niggas cook it up for you. Bring your ass on I got shit to do."

"Aight I'm on my way."

"Hurry up."

"1."

Tony walked into the bathroom while Me-Ka was taking a shower.

"You don't know how to knock?"

"I already seen it."

"So what."

"You wasn't that sexy before I got locked up."

"I was the same way. You was just blinded by Tanya."

Smiling.

"Whatever."

Getting out of the shower.

"You still going where you gotta go?"

"Yeah."

"You want me to drive you?"

"Yeah you can do that."

"Aight. Get out so I can get dressed."

"I can't watch you?"

"No. Get out."

Tony walked out of the bathroom packed his clothes up and watched TV while he waited for Me-Ka to get dress. When she was finished getting dress they checked out the room and Me-Ka drove to New Brighton. She pulled up in front of 456 Richmond Terrace Tony's new office.

"You got another class today?"

"Yeah but it don't start to 12:30."

"What you doing tonight?"

"Nothing. Why what up?"

"Lets go get something to eat later on."

"Aight. But we can't be out in the open like that."

"Don't worry about it. We can go somewhere on the low."

"Aight call me later."

"I'm gonna buy a cell phone today. When I get the number I'm gonna call you so you can save it."

"Aight."

Handing her a ten-dollar bill.

"Here take this get something eat."

"Nah I'm straight. I'm gonna go to my crib and wait for my class to start I'll make something to eat."

"You sure?"

"Yeah."

"I'll call you later on then."

Tony got out of Me-Ka's car and walked into the building thinking how good her pussy was. He took the elevator to the sixth floor and went to his new office 6B. Tony knocked on the door and Knowledge let him in. Greeting him with a hug. Tony noticed three dudes at the table working.

"What up nigga?"

"Shit I'm chilling."

"Welcome home."

"Good looking."

"I gotta be out so let me put you on how its gonna go down. Here put this mask on so you don't smell that shit and get high. Watch them they're almost finished cooking; they're gonna bag up for you. Make sure you watch them though, they are fiends they got sticky fingers. When they finish bagging up give them each two bags and kick them out. Believe me they will be back with every fiend in New Brighton. Give all the work to the dude in the back. He's gonna be in the house making the sells. You're gonna be up stairs in a fiend's house with the money. Every hour come down here collect the money and be out. Go back up stairs and count the money. There's gonna be three dudes in the house working for you. There's gonna be a dude in the back making the sells, there's gonna be a dude answering the door and there's gonna be another nigga kicking the fiends out after they finish smoking. You don't have to worry about these dudes stealing they already know I'm the enforcer. Stay here and watch them bag up. Let me get the dudes in the back so I can introduce you to them."

Knowledge walked into the back bedroom and returned with three grimy looking young kids.

"Yo this is my man Tony. Tony this is my trigger-happy crew. This is Jason, Keith and Young Blood. If somebody is stupid enough to try and run up in your spot believe me these niggas will handle it."

"Aight."

"Make sure yall hold my man down."

"If he's your family he's our family. Don't worry about it he's good."

"No question."

"Yo I gotta be out. One of yall watch the fiends so I can take Tony up stairs to the crib."

"Aight."

"He'll be right back."

Knowledge and Tony walked out of the apartment and into the staircase. They walked up one flight to the seventh floor to the fiend's house where Tony would be watching the money. Knowledge gave Tony the set of keys and they walked in the apartment.

"Check it this is basically your crib. The fiend is really strung out she's never gonna be here. All you gotta do is pay her $100 a month. She's on welfare so they pay her rent. Make sure you stay here and watch the money. I know you gonna want to be in the streets but just be easy. Grind for a minute then you can shine. This two for five shit is gonna make you a lot of money.

"I know. I already did the math."

Knowledge walked to the couch reached in the cushion pulled out a stainless steal .45 and handed it to Tony.

"Here keep this on you every time you go pick up that money. Be smart with it."

"Aight."

"I got a phone for you too. I know you gonna want to talk to them bitches."

"You know it."

"I'm gonna come back here like 3:00. Have that money counted because that brick you got down stairs will be gone before tomorrow."

"You think its gonna be gone that fast?"

"My nigga two for five is gonna have these fiends smoking like mad Russians."

"I hope so."

"I gotta get out of here. Go down stairs and let's get this shit cracking."

Chapter 27

As the day went on Tony couldn't believe how fast his work was moving. Every time he went to make a pick up there was a house full of fiends. He witnessed a fiend attempt to smoke $200 worth of crack. He shook his head at the fiend but took the money out of her hand. While in his spot he saw familiar faces that he had no idea they smoked. He even saw a kid he went to school with putting crack in his weed. "This crack shit ain't no joke". Later that evening Knowledge came through, they kicked it for a while and they both agreed upon the price that Knowledge would sell the bricks to Tony for. Tony thought Knowledge was looking out for him by setting the spot up but his real motive was to expand his business to New Brighton. Knowledge was already killing the streets in West Brighton by setting the spot up for Tony in New Brighton. He had no choice but to buy the bricks from Knowledge. Tony bought another brick from Knowledge and brought it downstairs so the three fiends could cook and bag it up for him. He paid Young Blood to watch them bag up for him because he was going to get something to eat with Me-Ka. He gave the trigger-happy crew fifty dollars and told them to order something to eat. He paid the three fiends thirty dollars each because he knew they were gonna smoke it up in his spot. At 9:00 he left out the building and got in Me-Ka's car.

"How you doing?"

Pulling off.

"I'm good. I'm just tired. How was your day?"

"I had a long day."

"What was you doing?"

"I didn't want to tell you on the phone but I got a little crack spot in the building."

"What! You better be careful boy."

"Nah I'm good. It's just for a little while so I can get on my feet."

"That's what they all say. I'm gonna get in and get out. They whine up making careers out of it."

"Not me. I'm going back to school."

"I hope so."

"Yo where we going?"

"To Applebee's by the mall."

"Why we going all the way out there?"

"The streets is watching."

"I ain't with all this creeping shit. I don't give a fuck whose watching."

"Stop fronting because you know you don't want Tanya or Ice to see us together."

"If they do see us they know we cool. They ain't gonna trip."

"It sounds good."

"Whatever. Yo I'm gonna need you to do me a favor some time tomorrow."

"What?"

"If I give you some money can you go buy me some clothes?"

"You should just come with me."

"Nah I'm on a grind. I didn't even want to leave now but I was thinking about you all day."

"So you say."

"That's my word you was on mind my all day."

"Me and what other chick?"

"There you go. You trying to tell me you didn't think about me today?"

"Nah I thought about you."

"What you thought about?"

"Tell you the truth I was thinking about how you beat it up last night."

"Yeah I did do my thing huh?"

"Whatever because you know you couldn't hold on when I was throwing it back."

"You gotta give me mines. Being backed up for a year I held my own."

"Nah you did."

"Word. You still didn't answer my question."

Pulling up in front of Applebee's.

"What?"

"Can you pick me up some clothes?"

"Oh yeah that ain't no problem. I wanted to pick up some shoes for the party anyway."

"What party?"

"This kid Mex is throwing a party at the Elks Club on Friday."

"I thought that was the death trap."

Walking into the restaurant.

"Nah I heard its been aight the last couple of weeks."

"Word if Ice go I'm in there."

"You know your girl Tanya is gonna be there."

"Stop calling her my girl. You my girl."

Laughing. "Says who?"

"What you trying to say you wouldn't be my girl?"

"It takes more than some good dick and dinner for me to be somebody's girl."

"That's only the beginning. There's more to come."

"We'll see when it gets here."

Having a seat in a booth.

"Aight but yo when the last time you seen my daughter?"

"I only seen her once since she been home from the hospital."

"Word I thought Tanya was your home girl."

"I haven't really fucked with her since she moved out my house."

"Why not?"

"My moms was nice enough to let her stay with us rent free. The day she moved out she didn't say thank you for anything. Christmas came no card in the mail, nothing. She don't even call my moms to say, "hey how you doing?". I can't fuck with her like that."

"Shit I feel you. Who the baby look like?"

"She looks just like you. Spitting image."

"She must be a fly little girl."

"Oh God. Who told you, you was fly?"

"Stop acting like that."

"Nah the little girl is cute but Money B going around telling people that's his daughter."

"Get the fuck out of here."

"I heard that from three different people."

"Yeah aight. That motherfucker is gonna make me knock his head off his shoulders."

"Don't get into it with him. Just see your baby and that's it."

"When you talk to that bitch ask her when can I see mines?"

"I'll see what she says."

"Why you say it like that?"

"I just ain't trying to get in the middle of yall situation."

"You ain't getting in the middle of nothing. Matter of fact I'll see her at the party. I'll ask her myself."

Tony and Me-Ka chatted over dinner. It disgusted Me-Ka how much she was feeling Tony's company. They both knew what they were doing was wrong but they rolled with the punches. After they ate Me-Ka drove back to New Brighton happy they weren't spotted by anybody.

"Where you want me to drop you off at?"

"Back at the building."

"Where you staying at?"

"Right now I'm gonna be staying at this fiends house until I do my thing enough to get an apartment."

"What? That's what got you in trouble last time. I got my own apartment on Prospect. You can stay with me for a minute if you want."

"Tell me the truth. You really concerned about the kid or you just want to keep me close."

Smiling. "Both."

"Aight check it let me go in the building handle something then I will call you. If you not sleep I'll come up there."

"I'm not gonna be sleep. I have to go in the house and study."

"Aight. I'm gonna take a cab up there because I now how you like to creep."

"I ain't creeping I'm just keeping people out of my business."

"So you say."

"Whatever call me when you on your way."

"Aight."

Tony went up stairs to find a house full of fiends getting high and the trigger-happy crew hemming somebody up. When he got them off the kid he realized it was his man he was locked up with, Pistol Pete.

"Yo chill out that's my man. What happened?"

"The nigga was coming through here all day. We thought he was a stick-up kid or something."

"Nah this is my man."

"We didn't know. We never seen the nigga before."

"Aight. Good looking for holding me down. Yo Pete do me a favor wait for me downstairs in the lobby. "

"Aight."

When Pete left out the apartment Jason and Keith went in the back room and Young Blood watched the door. Jason and Keith showed Tony the works that the fiends bagged up and gave him a backpack of full of money.

"Yall niggas straight?"

"We good."

"Yall ate right?"

"Yeah we ordered some Chinese food from around the corner."

"Knowledge told yall I was gonna take care of yall at the end of the week right?"

"Yeah we straight we know how it goes down. We always set Knowledge's spots up for him."

"Yo I'm gonna put the dude Pete on. He's gonna be in here so yall can rotate. If yall wanna go outside and get some fresh air or something he'll relieve you. Smelling this shit all day ain't good for you."

"Don't put him in here if he ain't gonna bust his gun if it gotta go down."

"Nah the nigga name Pistol Pete. His shit goes off."

"His name sounds good but we just had him hemmed up. He didn't have a burner on him."

"He was just up north with me he probably don't have a hammer yet."

"God you gotta get him a burner before you put him in here with us."

"Aight that's peace."

Tony took the bag of money up stairs stashed it and went to the lobby to kick it with Pistol Pete. When he got to the lobby Pete was in the lobby looking stressed.

"Yo what up nigga?"

"It ain't nothing. I'm ready to get some paper."

"How you find me so quick?"

"Fiends was talking about that two for five all the way in Park Hill. I knew it was you killing them."

"Get the fuck out of here."

"The word is out already. You turned it up real quick."

"Check it let them finish the night off. Come through tomorrow morning and I'll put you in the house. I gotta get you a burner because them niggas in there are trigger-happy."

"Aight."

"Yo you gotta be ready to bust your gun if it gotta go down."

"Nigga what's my name?"

"I hear you but them niggas are holding me down."

"Don't sweat it I got you."

"Aight come through tomorrow."

"Good looking."

Pete left out the building and Tony went up stairs to count the money. He left enough money in his stash to cop two bricks from Knowledge. He took the rest of the money in the cab with him to Me-Ka's house. On his ride to Me-Ka's house he stopped at the store to get some condoms so him and Me-Ka could get it poppin. Throughout the night he realized Me-Ka wanted more from him than just sex, so he didn't push to use the magnums. Me-Ka had plans of settling down with him although they each had baggage. The next morning Tony left out of her apartment before the birds chirped. He left a note for her to take money out the book bag to buy him some clothes, buy herself something nice and to hold on to the rest of the money for him. Tony walked from her apartment to his building thinking who else he could trust to work his spot. Other than Ice his mind drew a blank. When Tony walked in his spot he realized it was the first time he seen the spot empty. He was also surprised to see that all three of his soldiers were wide-awake.

"Yall on your job huh?"

"24-7."

"Tell the truth you thought you was gonna catch us off guard?"

"Yeah I did."

"Nah kid we are built for this."

"I respect that. Yall got some money for me?"

"Yeah its like twenty five hundred in that bag right there."

"Good looking. Yall got enough work for today?"

"We're good for a minute but later on tonight your gonna need another brick."

"Aight I'm gonna bring it back later on. I'll be up stairs if yall need me."

Tony left out the apartment. He went up stairs to count the money in the stash and added the twenty five hundred. He fell asleep on the sofa astonished how much and how fast the money was coming in.

Chapter 28

      The next couple of days Tony performed his daily operations to the drug game. Everything was running smoothly and he was living the life. He got dressed at Me-Ka's house for the party at the Elk's Club. Me-Ka dropped him off at the corner of Ice's crib because they were still doing the creeping thing. Like always Ice wasn't ready to leave when Tony got there. Tony shot pool as he waited for Ice to finish getting dressed. When Ice finally got ready for the spotlight they rode to the Elks comparing their weekly sells. Both swearing they made the most money. When they reached the club they both put their burners under the seat knowing how dudes hated to see them shine. As soon as they walked up to the door all eyes were on them. They paid the bouncers so they wouldn't have to wait on the ridiculous line. As they made their way through the crowded dance floor they heard whispering like they were celebrities. Most of the attention was on Tony because he had just come home and he was getting it in the streets. Also because of the outfit he had on. Me-Ka had gone shopping for him in Queens and picked him up Crème suede Mathew Deasia suit with brown leather stitching. A fresh shape up from Sean completed the outfit. He definitely made a serious first impression to the club scene. Throughout the night he and Ice received numerous compliments from their fans. As the party started winding down he spotted Money B and Tanya walk into the club. He thought he was over her but the site of them together made his blood boil. Tony stopped partying and kept his eye on them from across the dance floor. The first chance he had catching Tanya away from Money B he approached her. She thought she saw a ghost when he stepped in front of her as she tried to walk into the restroom.

Although Ice was tipsy he held Tony down. He kept his eye on Money B the whole time.

      "What up yo?"

Shocked.

"Excuse me. I'm trying to go to the bathroom."

"While you in the club who's watching Destiny?"

"My mother has her."

"I heard your bitch ass boyfriend is telling people that's his seed."

"He takes care of her."

"Let me hear that shit one more time from somebody in the street."

"Whatever."

"When can I come see her?"

"You can't."

Raising his voice, "I'll smack the shit out of you. Fuck you mean I can't see my daughter?"

This caught Money B's attention as he sped his way through the crowd. He would've had the drop on Tony but Ice stepped right in front of him.

"I know you ain't try to snuff my man."

"This shit ain't got nothing to do with you Ice."

"So what that's my man."

By this time Tony had turned around realizing Money B and Ice was getting into it. Not saying any words Tony stepped around Ice and punched Money B in the jaw. He staggered a little bit. Before Money B could retaliate the lights came on in the club and the biggest bouncers working were pushing Tony and Ice out of the club. Money B's manhood being assaulted he started throwing threats in the air towards Tony. Ice and Tony ran to the car with every attention of finishing Money B when he walked out the club, but when they got back in front of the club the party was over and the club was emptying out. They both agreed there were too many witnesses for the DEA. Tony and Ice drove back to New Brighton promising each other they had to lay Money B down. When Ice dropped Tony off at his building Me-Ka called his cell phone in a frenzy worrying about him.

"Hello."

"You aight?"

"Yeah I'm good. It ain't nothing."

"Where you at?"

"I just got to the building."

"You staying with me tonight?"

"Yeah. I'll be over there in a minute. Let me do my thing real quick."

"Alright. I'll be in the house waiting for you"

"Aight 1."

Tony went in the building to warn his four soldiers to be on their job. He called them all into the back room and told them what went down at the club.

"Check it. He got a little stick-up crew so I need yall to be alert."

"We always alert."

"I know but for real he's a grimy nigga."

"Who's the dude?"

"The nigga Money B from Stapelton."

"He mess with your baby moms right?"

"Yeah."

"For the right price he'll be floating in that water across the street."

"Nah I gotta handle this one but if he tries to come up in here I want yall to put some slugs in him."

"Nigga if anybody tries to come in here they gonna get it."

"Aight then. Yall got that paper for me?"

"Yeah its right here."

Tony counted out two g's and gave them each five hundred. The trigger-happy crew was grateful because Knowledge never paid them that much for a week. Pistol Pete was excited because that was the first paper he made since he'd been home and he was home a month before Tony. Tony took the rest of the money he collected and brought it upstairs. He put it in the stash and called a cab so he could go to his second home. Tony went downstairs and waited in front the building for a cab. While he waited for the cab a Honda Accord pulled up in front of the building. Two dudes got out the car and started letting off at Tony. He had to think quickly because the building door was locked. Tony pulled his hammer out and started blazing back. When the two dudes realized he wasn't letting up they jumped back in the car and the driver drove off. A few moments later Tony walked to his cab as three of his soldiers ran out the building ready to shed blood.

"You straight?"

"Yeah I'm good. Faggot ass niggas was shooting at the wall."

"You saw who it was?"

"Nah but them niggas was in a Honda Accord."

"A white one with tinted windows?"

"Yeah."

"That's the nigga Money B whip."

"Aight. Here take this burner; give me yours just in case I see them niggas again. Hit me on my cell if anything goes down."

"Aight."

"If not I'll see yall niggas tomorrow."

Tony rode in the cab dialing Ice's number to make sure they didn't get at him. The cab driver rode past Ice's house. His truck wasn't parked so he left a message for him to call him right away. Tony used his keys to get into Me-Ka's house. She was sitting in the living room with her coat still on in a panic.

"What's wrong with you?"

"I was worried about you."

"You don't have to worry about me I'm good."

"How did that shit start at the club?"

"I was talking to Tanya and I guess he tried to snuff me because when I turned around him and Ice was getting into it. I stepped in front of Ice and tried to take Money B's head off.

"You know it's not over right?"

"I know. Them niggas was just shooting at me."

"When?"

"When I was waiting for the cab in front of the building."

"Who was it?"

"I don't know but them niggas was soft. I didn't have nowhere to run and them clowns were shooting at the wall."

"What was you doing when they were shooting at you?"

"I was playing duck hunt. I was trying to kill one of them niggas."

"Tony you changed since you got locked up."

"How you figure?"

"The old Tony was nice and sweet this new Tony is a gangster."

"I ain't no gangster I'm a survivor."

"Who you think you are Beyonce?"

"You a funny girl. Nah I do what it takes to get by."

"Just be safe."

"I told you I'm good." giving Me-ka a kiss. "You can't tell me I'm not a sweetheart to you."

"I ain't complaining." getting on her knees and unbuckling Tony's pants.

Tony leaned back on the sofa and let Me-ka do her thing. She removed his sedated cock from his boxers and inserted it into her mouth. Within seconds she made his pipe erect. Tony enjoyed her gentle strokes until he thirsts.

"Yo get naked."

Me-ka undressed with ease all she had on was a cat suit. She went to have a seat on his erection but he stopped her.

"Nah come put it in my face."

They lay on the sofa in a sixty-nine position providing oral sexual favors to each other. After a while Tony stopped and watched Me-Ka have convulsions on his pipe. When he felt his ejaculation progressing he warned her but she insisted that he explode in her mouth. When he did explode she had a daycare in her throat. Tony again laid on the sofa experiencing after shock. While Me-Ka waited for him to pull his self together she sat on the sofa and masturbated. Tony took longer than she thought to recover. Me-Ka played with her clitoris until she reached her pinnacle. She joined Tony in the after shock stage. Later that evening Tony massaged Fredrick of Hollywood body oil onto her back until she fell asleep. Shortly there after his cell phone rang he just knew something had happened.

"Hello."

"Yo what happened?"

"I was calling to make sure you was good."

"Yeah I'm straight."

"That clown ass nigga had some dudes shoot at me."

"When?"

"I was in front of the building right before I called you."

"Say word, what was you doing outside?"

Not wanting to tell him he was going to see Me-Ka.

"I was waiting for a cab to go to White Castles."

"You had your hammer on you?"

"You know it. I was blazing right back at them clowns."

"That nigga gotta get it soon."

"Who you telling. If I see him in church he's getting it right there."

"Fuck it where you at now?"

"I'm in the crib about to go to sleep."

"Aight then get at me in the morning."

"Smooth."

"Water."

Tony hung up the phone looking at Me-Ka sleeping hoping she wouldn't come between him and his man Ice. He snuggled next to her and fell asleep.

Chapter 29

For the next couple of months everything was quiet for Tony. He didn't have any run ins with Money B and his operation was progressing. Tony was able to persuade Me-Ka to put an Infiniti in her name for him. He bought the car from a fiend so he didn't pay that much for it but he put a lot of money into it. Tony had one of the hottest cars on the Island. It was summer time so he felt it was his time to shine. He wanted to give back to the community so one Saturday he sponsored a basketball tournament in Mahoney Park. During the day he had a barbecue for the kids in the neighborhood and at night he had an all you can drink gathering in the park for the adults. That night was the first time all summer the Trilogy (Tony, Ice, and Knowledge) was able to kick it with each other.

"Yo Ice this little young nigga came home and turned it up in the hood."
"This nigga Tony used to be scared to sell candy for school. Now he out here selling crack and making a killing."
"I don't know what the fuck yall niggas talking about. I'm hurting."
"This nigga think he Nino Brown or meals on wheels feeding the neighborhood."
"Tell you the truth I was watching New Jack City the other day and I was like fuck it I'm gonna do that shit."
"Fuck is this your one good deed to the community?"
"Most of the motherfuckers in the park are my customers and the rest of them are snitches so I need them to be on my side."
"I feel you."
"Look at the nigga shinning. His car is fresh and look at the ice in the nigga ear.
"I don't do much."

"You doing something. Niggas in the streets is calling you Nicky Barnes of Staten Island."

"Nah I'm chilling."

"But yo on some real shit the streets is talking."

"Fuck you talking about Knowledge?"

"You gotta be careful out here. A couple people told me Money B got his money right and he got some paper work on your head."

"God I ain't sweating that nigga."

"Just be alert."

"For real God don't sleep. Niggas in the streets was clowning him for a minute about you almost knocking him out in the Elks that night."

"Yeah I know."

"Tony I'm not telling you to stop living just be aware of your surrounds."

"I know that's why I always got that thing with me."

"Yeah keep that with you."

"Fuck it though. Yall niggas going to Zodokos tonight."

"Nah I ain't fucking with it."

"I ain't fucking with that shit either. It's too small in there."

"I told my team I'll go out with them tonight."

"You still got the trigger-happy crew working for you?"

"Hell yeah. I pay them niggas well."

"Yeah keep them. They are some good niggas to have around. They tore West Brighton up for me one night. They shot up the whole projects."

"Yeah I got them three and this dude I was locked up with, Pistol Pete. Them four niggas together will shut Staten Island down if I told them to. Ice I'm telling you, you need a crew like that."

"I don't be sweating that gun shit. Let me get my money and that's it. A nigga cross me I'm gonna handle it right there and that's it."

"And that's why I fucks with you Ice. But yo Tone, Ice let me get out of here yall niggas be safe in these streets."

"Yeah Knowledge I'm about to get out this park with you. I know my girl is in the crib beefing. I was supposed to pick her up an hour ago."

Knowledge and Ice left out the park; Tony stuck around and accepted praises from the adults in the neighborhood. After the liquor was gone people started leaving out of the park. Tony got in his car and made his way to Me-Ka's apartment. He thought a car was following him but he paid it no mind. Tony figured it was his mind playing tricks on him because the Hennessy he was sipping had him woozy. When he got in the house Me-Ka was putting on an outfit to wear that night.

"Where you going?"

"My friend from school wants to go to the movies but I don't feel like it."

"Yall should just got to Zodokos."

"Nah she's stuck up she ain't gonna like it in there."

"Yeah yall perfect for each other."

"Why you say that?"

"Yall both stuck up."

"Whatever."

"Nah I'm only playing you ain't stuck up baby girl." Giving her a kiss on her forehead.

"You was drinking?"

"Yeah I had a sip of Hennessy."

"You a fucking alcoholic."

"Here we go again."

"It's true. You can't be somewhere without drinking."

"Do me a favor."

"What?"

"Pick me out something to wear."

"Why don't you just wear what you got on?"

"I had this on all day. Niggas already seen me in this."

"And. Everybody that was at the park is going straight to the party. Ain't nobody changing."

"That's why I'm changing. I'm on a higher level than them."

"Whatever. Here wear this and no I am not ironing it." Passing him a St. John's throwback and a pair of jeans."

"Nobody was gonna ask you to iron it."

"Oh yeah your girlfriend Tanya called me. She said if I see you to tell you she needs some money for Destiny."

"I told you stop calling her my girlfriend and I just gave that bitch money the other day."

"I told you. You keep giving she's gonna keep asking."

"I ain't giving her shit."

"Yeah right. I already know how its gonna go down. She's gonna see you outside, ask you for some money you're gonna say no and she's gonna make a scene. You're gonna get tired of her and give her the money. It happens every time."

"Not this time."

"So you say. You soft. She be playing you."

"If I'm so soft why you with me?"

Wrapping her arms around him.

"Because you my soft baby and I love you."

"Whatever man get away from me."

Later that night they left out the house together and went their separate ways. Me-Ka met her friend at the movies and Tony met his team at Zodokos. When Me-Ka and her friend got to the movies there was nothing playing they wanted to see. They both decided to call it a night and go home. On Me-Ka's drive home she rode up Victory Boulevard passed by Zodokos seen that it was crowded and parked in KFC's parking lot. She promised herself that she would only stay for a half-hour because she knew niggas did not know how to act in there. When she got inside the club she seen Tony and his crew at the bar doing their thing. As she was mingling in the crowd she saw Tanya at a table with some girls from Stapelton. She had a seat at the table with them facing the bar, so she could see if Tony tried to creep with another chick. As the night went on she realized that one of the dudes in Tony's crew kept giving him drinks. By 2:00 he was pissy drunk. Tony got up off the bar stole and walked off towards the bathroom. When he walked off the dude that was giving him all the drinks walked away from the bar towards the front door? Tony walked into the bathroom and a dude that was standing in the corner followed him into the bathroom. It was so packed in the club Me-Ka couldn't see who the guy was that followed him into the bathroom. After a few minutes when Tony didn't come out the bathroom Me-Ka knew something was up. She excused herself from the table and made her way to the bathroom. When she got there the lights were off and she heard tussling. She pushed the door open and felt against the wall for the light switch. When she flicked the lights on there was Tony and Money B in there getting it on. Tony must've knocked a gun out of Money B's hand because it was on the floor next to the sink and they were scuffling in between the toilet stall.

When Me-Ka first walked in the bathroom Tony was holding his own but being that he was drunk Money B started to get the best of him. Money B was fucking Tony up in the stall, while he was getting his ass beat Tony was able to grab Money B's face to bite him. He was trying to take a chunk out of his cheek, while Tony was chewing at his cheek Money B reached in his back pocket and grabbed a razor. He swung the razor and it caught Tony on the back of his neck. The pain from the cut made him release Money B and Money B swung the razor again cutting Tony in his face. That cut sent a shock down Me-Ka's spine and she picked the black 9mm off the floor. Money B had his back towards her ready to swing the razor again when she let off the first shot. The slug hit him in his back and he fell instantly on his side. She pulled the trigger again and emptied the remains of the clip into his corpse. The gun shots sobered Tony and he jumped up off the floor. Me-Ka stood over Money B's body in shock. All cut up he grabbed the gun from his girl's hand and dragged her out of the bathroom. When they got out the bathroom the music had stopped and people was fleeing the club but there were some eyes on them. Pistol Pete stood outside the club on his cell phone calling the police. Tony walked Me-Ka to her car and told her to go straight home. He tried to make his way to St. Vincent's hospital to get stitched up but before he could make a left on Castleton Avenue once again he seen those red lights flashing behind him. He didn't have any energy left in him for a chase so he pulled over right there. Before the detectives could get to him in the car he had passed out. They rushed him to the hospital where he was placed under arrest for the death of Melvin Jackson. At the club Tanya and Pistol Pete cooperated with the police while photographers took pictures of Money B's body stretched out in a pool of blood.

Chapter 30

       The day of Tony's arraignment Mrs. Clark, Me-Ka and Ice sat together in the courtroom listening to Pistol Pete testify against Tony. The DEA had a talking witness and the murder weapon; Tony knew he was going down he just hoped the judge didn't throw football numbers at him. The DEA offered him a deal because although the gun was retrieved from his car they found other fingerprints on the gun. His deal was six months in jail for violating his parole if he snitched on Knowledge in his drug case. He adamantly turned down the deal knowing he could never betray his friendship with Knowledge. Tony wouldn't be able to live with himself if he took that deal. Tony sat in the courtroom in disgust listening to Pistol Pete testify against him after he took him under his wing when they were up north. Tony even gave him a job once he got on his feet. The jury deliberated the case for two hours and they found him guilty on two charges; Murder in the first degree and possession of an illegal firearm. The judge could've given him 25-life but being that he was tender in age the judge gave him 15-25 years with the chance of parole in 10. When Mrs. Clark heard Tony's charge she almost fainted. Ice grabbed her and walked her out of the courtroom. Me-Ka stayed seated as the court officer escorted Tony out of the courtroom. Before he left out he looked Me-Ka in her face and whispered I love you. During Tony's incarceration he interacted with all types of criminals, murderers, rapists, arsonists and now his time has come. As he walks through the gates towards freedom he's happy to say that he served his time as a Scrambler.

The life is good, but is it worth it ?